PUFFIN BOOKS

Thirteen Unpredictable Tales

Paul Jennings was born in England in 1943 and emigrated to Australia aged six. The trip for the family cost ten pounds – the Australian government paid the rest of the fare in those days.

Paul taught disabled and socially deprived children for six years and then worked as a speech therapist. He later lectured in special education before his appointment as Senior Lecturer in Language and Literature at the Warrnambool Institute, where he worked for ten years before becoming a full-time writer in 1989.

Paul's stories are funny, weird and wacky with surprising endings. He wants all children to have their noses in the same books and reluctant readers to discover that reading is fun. 'Books are fantastic. That's what I want my readers to think.'

Since *Unreal!* was published in 1985, Paul's books have sold over two million copies. He has won many 'Children's Choice' awards and in January 1995 was awarded the Medal of the Order of Australia for Services to Children's Literature.

PAUL JENNINGS

THIRTEEN

Unpredictable

TALES

A collection of his best stories chosen by Wendy Cooling

PUFFIN BOOKS

PUFFIN BOOKS

Published by the Penguin Group
Penguin Books Ltd, 80 Strand, London WC2R 0RL, England
Penguin Putnam Inc., 375 Hudson Street, New York, New York 10014, USA
Penguin Books Australia Ltd, 250 Camberwell Road, Camberwell, Victoria 3124, Australia
Penguin Books Canada Ltd, 10 Alcorn Avenue, Toronto, Ontario, Canada M4V 3B2
Penguin Books India (P) Ltd, 11 Community Centre, Panchsheel Park, New Delhi – 110 017, India
Penguin Books (NZ) Ltd, Cnr Rosedale and Airborne Roads, Albany, Auckland, New Zealand
Penguin Books (South Africa) (Pty) Ltd, 24 Sturdee Avenue, Rosebank 2196, South Africa

Penguin Books Ltd, Registered Offices: 80 Strand, London WC2R 0RL, England

www.penguin.com

First published by Viking 1996
Published in Puffin Books 1997
14

'The Strap Box Flyer' and 'Wunderpants' first appeared in *Unreal!*
published by Penguin Books Australia 1985, copyright © Lockley Lodge Pty Ltd, 1985
'The Copy' and 'No is Yes' first appeared in *Quirky Tails*
published by Penguin Books Australia 1987, copyright © Lockley Lodge Pty Ltd, 1987
'Pink Bow Tie' and 'There's No Such Thing' first appeared in *Unbelievable!*
published by Penguin Books Australia 1987, copyright © Lockley Lodge Pty Ltd, 1986
'Spaghetti Pig-Out' first appeared in *Uncanny!*
published by Penguin Books Australia 1988, copyright © Lockley Lodge Pty Ltd, 1988
'Nails' and 'Only Gilt' first appeared in *Unbearable!*
published by Penguin Books Australia 1990, copyright © Lockley Lodge Pty Ltd, 1990
'Ex Poser' and 'Ice Maiden' first appeared in *Unmentionable!*
published by Penguin Books Australia 1991, copyright © Lockley Lodge Pty Ltd, 1991
'Clear as Mud' and 'Thought Full' first appeared in *Undone!*
published by Penguin Books Australia 1993, copyright © Lockley Lodge Pty Ltd, 1993

The moral right of the author has been asserted

Typeset in Berkeley

Made and printed in England by Clays Ltd, St Ives plc

British Library Cataloguing in Publication Data
A CIP catalogue record for this book is available from the British Library

ISBN 0–140–37790–5

Contents

Ex Poser

There are two rich kids in our form. Sandra Morris and Ben Fox. They are both snobs. They think they are too good for the rest of us. Their parents have big cars and big houses. Both of them are quiet. They keep to themselves. I guess they don't want to mix with the ruffians like me.

Ben Fox always wears expensive gym shoes and the latest fashions. He thinks he is good-looking with his blue eyes and blond hair. He is a real poser.

Sandra Morris is the same. And she knows it. Blue eyes and blonde hair too. Skin like silk. Why do some kids get the best of everything?

Me, I landed pimples. I've used everything I can on them. But still they bud and grow and burst. Just when you don't want them to. It's not fair.

Anyway, today I have the chance to even things up. Boffin is bringing along his latest invention – a lie detector. Sandra Morris is the victim. She agreed to try it out because everyone knows that she would never tell a lie. What she doesn't know is that Boffin and I are going to ask her some very embarrassing questions.

Boffin is a brain. His inventions always work. He is smarter than the teachers. Everyone knows that. And now he has brought along his latest effort. A lie detector.

He tapes two wires to Sandra's arm. 'It doesn't hurt,' he says. 'But it is deadly accurate.' He switches on the machine and a little needle swings into the middle of the dial. 'Here's a trial question,' he says. 'Are you a girl?'

Sandra nods.

'You have to say yes or no,' he says.

'Yes,' replies Sandra. The needle swings over to TRUTH. Maybe this thing really works. Boffin gives a big grin.

'This time tell a lie,' says Boffin. 'Are you a girl?' he asks again.

Sandra smiles with that lovely smile of hers. 'No,' she says. A little laugh goes up but then all the kids in the room gasp. The needle points to LIE. This lie detector is a terrific invention.

'OK,' says Boffin. 'You only have seven questions, David. The batteries will go flat after another seven questions.' He sits down behind his machine and twiddles the knobs.

This is going to be fun. I am going to find out a little bit about Sandra Morris and Ben Fox. It's going to be very interesting. Very interesting indeed.

I ask my first question. 'Have you ever kissed Ben Fox?'

Sandra goes red. Ben Fox goes red. I have got them this time. I am sure they have something going between them. I will expose them.

'No,' says Sandra. Everyone cranes their neck to see what the lie detector says. The needle points to TRUTH.

This is not what I expected. And I only have six questions left. I can't let her off the hook. I am going to expose them both.

'Have you ever held his hand?'

Again she says, 'No.' And the needle says TRUTH. I am starting to feel guilty. Why am I doing this?

I try another tack. 'Are you in love?' I ask.

A red flush starts to crawl up her neck. I am feeling really mean now. Fox is blushing like a sunset.

'Yes,' she says. The needle points to TRUTH.

3

I shouldn't have let the kids talk me into doing this. I decide to put Sandra and Ben out of their agony. I won't actually name him. I'll spare her that. 'Is he in this room?' I say.

She looks at the red Ben Fox. 'Yes,' she says. The needle points to TRUTH.

'Does he have blue eyes?' I ask.

'No,' she says.

'Brown?' I say.

'No,' she says again.

I don't know what to say next. I look at each kid in the class very carefully. Ben Fox has blue eyes. I was sure that she loved him.

'This thing doesn't work,' I say to Boffin. 'I can't see one kid who doesn't have either blue eyes or brown eyes.'

'We can,' says Boffin. They are all looking at me.

I can feel *my* face turning red now. I wish I could sink through the floor but I get on with my last question. 'Is he an idiot?' I ask.

Sandra is very embarrassed. 'Yes,' she says in a voice that is softer than a whisper. 'And he has green eyes.'

Spaghetti Pig-Out

Guts Garvey was a real mean kid. He made my life miserable. I don't know why he didn't like me. I hadn't done anything to him. Not a thing.

He wouldn't let any of the other kids hang around with me. I was on my own. Anyone in the school who spoke to me was in his bad books. I wandered around the yard at lunch time like a dead leaf blown in the wind.

I tried everything. I even gave him my pocket money one week. He just bought a block of chocolate from the canteen and ate it in front of me. Without even giving me a bit. What a rat.

After school I only had one friend. My cat – Bad Smell. She was called that because now and then she would make a bad smell. Well, she couldn't help it. Everyone has their faults. She was a terrific cat. But still. A cat is not enough. You need other kids for friends too.

Even after school no one would come near me. I only had one thing to do. Watch the television. But that wasn't much good either. There were only little kids' shows on before tea.

'I wish we had a video,' I said to Mum one night.

'We can't afford it, Matthew,' said Mum. 'Anyway, you watch too much television as it is. Why don't you go and do something with a friend?'

I didn't say anything. I couldn't tell her that I didn't have any friends. And never would have as long as Guts Garvey was around. A bit later Dad came in. He had a large parcel under his arm. 'What have you got, Dad?' I asked.

'It's something good,' he answered. He put the package on the lounge-room floor and I started to unwrap it. It was about the size of large cake. It was green and spongy with an opening in the front.

'What is it?' I said.

'What you've always wanted. A video player.'

I looked at it again. 'I've never seen video player like this before. It looks more like a mouldy loaf of bread with a hole in the front.'

'Where did you get it?' asked Mum in a dangerous voice. 'And how much was it?'

'I bought it off a bloke in the pub. A real bargain. Only fifty dollars.'

'Fifty dollars is cheap for a video,' I said. 'But is it a video? It doesn't look like one to me. Where are the cables?'

'He said it doesn't need cables. You just put in the video and press this.' He handed me a green thing that looked like a bar of chocolate with a couple of licorice blocks stuck on the top.

'You're joking,' I said. 'That's not a remote control.'

'How much did you have to drink?' said Mum. 'You must have been crazy to pay good money for that junk.' She went off into the kitchen. I could tell that she was in a bad mood.

'Well at least try it,' said Dad sadly. He handed me a video that he had hired down the street. It was called *Revenge of the Robots*. I pushed the video into the mushy hole and switched on the TV set. Nothing happened.

I looked at the licorice blocks on the green chocolate thing. It was worth a try. I pushed one of the black squares.

The movie started playing at once. 'It works,' I

yelled. 'Good on you, Dad. It works. What a ripper.'

Mum came in and smiled. 'Well what do you know,' she said. 'Who would have thought that funny-looking thing was a video set? What will they think of next?'

2

Dad went out and helped Mum get tea while I sat down and watched the movie. I tried out all the licorice-like buttons on the remote control. One was for fast forward, another was pause and another for rewind. The rewind was good. You could watch all the people doing things backwards.

I was rapt to have a video but to tell the truth the movie was a bit boring. I started to fiddle around with the handset. I pointed it at things in the room and pressed the buttons. I pretended that it was a ray gun.

'Tea time,' said Mum after a while.

'What are we having?' I yelled.

'Spaghetti,' said Mum.

I put the video on pause and went to the door. I was just about to say, 'I'm not hungry,' when I noticed something. Bad Smell was sitting staring at the TV in a funny way. I couldn't figure out what it was at first but I could see that something was wrong. She was so still. I had never seen a cat sit so still before. Her tail didn't swish. Her eyes didn't blink. She just sat there like a statue. I took off my thong and threw it over near her. She didn't move. Not one bit. Not one whisker.

'Dad,' I yelled. 'Something is wrong with Bad Smell.'

He came into the lounge and looked at the poor cat. It sat there staring up at the screen with glassy eyes. Dad waved his hand in front of her face. Nothing. Not a blink. 'She's dead,' said Dad.

'Oh no,' I cried. 'Not Bad Smell. Not her. She can't be. My only friend.' I picked her up. She stayed in the sitting-up position. I put her back on the floor. No change. She sat there stiffly. I felt for a pulse but I couldn't feel one. Her chest wasn't moving. She wasn't breathing.

'Something's not quite right,' said Dad. 'But I can't figure out what it is.'

'She shouldn't be sitting up,' I yelled. 'Dead cats don't sit up. They fall over with their legs pointed up.'

Dad picked up Bad Smell and felt all over her. 'It's no good, Matthew,' he said. 'She's gone. We will bury her in the garden after tea.' He patted me on the head and went into the kitchen.

Tears came into my eyes. I hugged Bad Smell to my chest. She wasn't stiff. Dead cats should be stiff. I remembered a dead cat that I once saw on the footpath. I had picked it up by the tail and it hadn't bent. It had been like picking up a saucepan by the handle.

Bad Smell felt soft. Like a toy doll. Not stiff and hard like the cat on the footpath.

Suddenly I had an idea. I don't know what gave it to me. It just sort of popped into my head. I picked up the funny-looking remote control, pointed it at Bad Smell and pressed the FORWARD button. The cat blinked, stretched, and stood up. I pressed PAUSE again and she froze. A statue again. But this time she was standing up.

I couldn't believe it. I rubbed my eyes. The pause button was working on my cat. I pressed FORWARD a second time and off she went. Walking into the kitchen as if nothing had happened.

Dad's voice boomed out from the kitchen. 'Look. Bad Smell is alive.' He picked her up and examined her. 'She must have been in a coma. Just as well we didn't bury her.' Dad had a big smile on his face. He put Bad Smell down and shook his head. I went back to the lounge.

I hit one of the licorice-like buttons. None of them had anything written on them but by now I knew what each of them did.

Or I thought I did.

3

The movie started up again. I watched it for a while until a blow fly started buzzing around and annoying me. I pointed the handset at it just for fun and pressed FAST FORWARD. The fly vanished. Or that's what seemed to happen. It was gone from sight but I could still hear it. The noise was tremendous. It was like a tiny jet fighter screaming around in the room. I saw something flash by. It whipped past me again. And again. And again. The blow fly was going so fast that I couldn't see it.

I pushed the PAUSE button and pointed it up where the noise was coming from. The fly must have gone right through the beam because it suddenly appeared out of nowhere. It hung silently in mid air. Still. solidified. A floating, frozen fly. I pointed the handset at it again and pressed FORWARD. The blow fly came to life at once. It buzzed around the room at its normal speed.

'Come on,' yelled Mum. 'Your tea is ready.'

I wasn't interested in tea. I wasn't interested in anything except this fantastic remote control. It seemed to be able to make animals and insects freeze or go fast forward. I looked through the kitchen door at Dad. He had already started eating. Long pieces of spaghetti dangled from his mouth. He was chewing and sucking at the same time.

Now don't get me wrong. I love Dad. I always have. He is a terrific bloke. But one thing that he used to do really bugged me. It was the way he ate spaghetti. He sort of made slurping noises and the meat sauce gathered around his lips as he sucked. It used to get on my nerves. I think that's why I did what I did. I know it's a weak excuse. I shivered. Then I pointed the control at him and hit the PAUSE button.

Dad stopped eating. He turned rock solid and just sat there with the fork half way up to his lips. His mouth was wide open. His eyes stared. The spaghetti hung from his fork like worms of concrete. He didn't blink. He didn't move. He was as stiff as a tree trunk.

Mum looked at him and laughed. 'Good one,' she said. 'You'd do anything for a laugh, Arthur.'

Dad didn't move.

'OK,' said Mum. 'That's enough. You're setting a bad example for Matthew by fooling around with your food like that.'

My frozen father never so much as moved an eyeball. Mum gave him a friendly push on the shoulder and he started to topple. Over he went. He looked just like a statue that had been pushed off its mount. Crash. He lay on the ground. His hand still half way up to his mouth. The solid spaghetti hung in the same position. Only now it stretched out sideways pointing at his toes.

Mum gave a little scream and rushed over to him. Quick as a flash I pointed the remote control at him and pressed FORWARD. The spaghetti dangled downwards. Dad sat up and rubbed his head. 'What happened?' he asked.

'You had a little turn,' said Mum in a worried voice. 'You had better go straight down to the hospital and have a check up. I'll get the car. Matthew, you stay here and finish your tea. We won't be long.'

I was going to tell them about the remote control but something made me stop. I had a thought. If I told them about it they would take it off me. It was the last I would see of it for sure. If I kept it to myself

I could take it to school. I could show Guts Garvey my fantastic new find. He would have to make friends with me now that I had something as good as this. Every kid in the school would want to have a go.

Dad and Mum came home after about two hours. Dad went straight to bed. The doctor had told him to have a few days' rest. He said Dad had been working too hard. I took the remote control to bed with me. I didn't use it until the next day.

4

It was Saturday and I slept in. I did my morning jobs and set out to find Guts Garvey. He usually hung around the shops on Saturday with his tough mates.

The shopping centre was crowded. As I went I looked in the shop windows. In a small cafe I noticed a man and a woman having lunch. They were sitting at a table close to the window. I could see everything that they were eating. The man was having a steak and what was left of a runny egg. He had almost finished his meal.

It reminded me of Dad and the spaghetti. I took out the remote control and looked at it. I knew that it could do PAUSE, FORWARD and FAST FORWARD.

There was one more button. I couldn't remember what this last button was for. I pushed it.

I wouldn't have done it on purpose. I didn't really realize that it was pointing at the man in the shop. The poor thing.

The last button was REWIND.

Straight away he began to un-eat his meal. He went backwards. He put his fork up to his mouth and started taking out the food and placing it back on his plate. The runny egg came out of his mouth with bits of steak and chips. In, out, in, out, went his fork. Each time bringing a bit of food out of his mouth. He moved the mashed-up bits backwards on his plate with the knife and fork and they all formed up into solid chips, steak and eggs.

It was unbelievable. He was un-chewing his food and un-eating his meal. Before I could gather my wits his whole meal was back on the plate. He then put his clean knife and fork down on the table.

My head swirled but suddenly I knew what I had to do. I pressed FORWARD. Straight away he picked up his knife and fork and began to eat his meal for the second time. The woman sitting opposite him had pushed her fist up into her mouth. She was terrified. She didn't know what was going on.

Suddenly she screamed and ran out of the cafe. The man didn't take any notice he just kept eating. He had to eat the whole meal again before he could stop.

I ran down the street feeling as guilty as sin. This thing was powerful. It could make people do things backwards.

I stopped at the corner. There, talking to his mean mate Rabbit, was Guts Garvey. This was my big chance to get into his good books. 'Look,' I said. 'Take a squizz at this.' I held out the remote control.

Guts Garvey grabbed it from my hand. 'Yuck,' he growled. 'Green chocolate. Buzz off, bird brain.' He lifted up the remote control. He was going to throw it at me.

'No,' I yelled. 'It's a remote control. From a video. You press the black things.' Guts Garvey looked at me. Then he looked at the control. He didn't believe me but he pressed one of the buttons.

Rabbit was bouncing a basketball up and down on the footpath. He suddenly froze. So did the ball. Rabbit stood there on one leg and the ball floated without moving, half way between his hand and the ground. Guts Garvey's mouth dropped open. He rubbed his eyes and looked again. The statue of Rabbit was still there.

'Press FORWARD,' I said, pointing to the top button.

Guts pressed the control again and Rabbit finished bouncing the ball. I smiled. I could see that Guts was impressed. He turned and looked at me. Then he pointed the remote control straight at my face. 'No,' I screamed. 'No.'

But I was too late. Guts Garvey pressed the button. He 'paused' me. I couldn't move. I just stood there with both arms frozen up in the air. My eyes stared. They didn't move. Nothing moved. I was rock solid. Guts and Rabbit laughed. Then they ran off.

5

People gathered round. At first they laughed. A whole circle of kids and adults looking at the stupid dill standing there like a statue. Someone waved their hand in front of my face. A girl poked me. 'He's good,' said someone. 'He's not moving a muscle.'

I tried to speak. My mouth wouldn't move. My tongue wouldn't budge. The crowd got bigger. I felt an idiot. What a fool. Dozens of people were staring at me wondering why I was standing there posed like a picture on the wall. Then I stopped feeling stupid. I felt scared. What if I stayed like this for ever? Not breathing. Not moving. Not alive, not dead. What would they do with me? Put me in the garden like a garden gnome? Stash me away in a museum? Bury me alive? It was too terrible to think about.

Suddenly I collapsed. I puddled on to the ground. Everyone laughed. I stood up and ran off as fast as I could go. As I ran I tried to figure it out. Why had I suddenly gone off pause? Then I realized what it was. I remembered my Uncle Frank's video. If you put it on pause and went away it would start up again automatically after three or four minutes. The movie would come off pause and keep going. That's what had happened to me.

I looked ahead. I could just make out two tiny figures in the distance. It was Rabbit and Guts Garvey. With my remote control. I had to get it back. The dirty rats had nicked it. I didn't care about getting in Guts Garvey's good books any more. I just wanted my controller back.

And revenge. I wanted revenge.

I ran like a mad thing after them.

It was no good. I was out of breath and they were too far away. I couldn't catch them. I looked around. Shaun Potter, a kid from school, was sitting on his horse, Star, on the other side of the road. I rushed over to him. 'Help,' I said. 'You've got to help. Guts Garvey has pinched my remote control. I've got to get it back. It's a matter of life and death.'

Shaun looked at me. He wasn't a bad sort of kid. He was one of the few people in the school who had been kind to me. He wasn't exactly a friend. He was too scared of Guts Garvey for that. But I could tell by the way he smiled and nodded at me that he liked me. I jumped from foot to foot. I was beside myself. I had to get that remote control back. Shaun hesitated for a second or two. Then he said, 'OK, hop up.'

I put one foot in the stirrup and Shaun pulled me up behind him on to Star's back. 'They went that way,' I yelled.

Star went into a trot and then a canter. I held on for grim death. I had never been on a horse before. I bumped up and down behind Shaun. The ground seemed a long way down. I was scared but I didn't say anything. I had to catch Guts Garvey and Rabbit. We sped down the street past all the parked cars and people crossing the road.

'There they are,' I yelled. Guts and Rabbit were in a line of people waiting for a bus. Shaun slowed Star down to a walk. Guts Garvey looked up and saw us.

He pulled the remote control from his pocket. 'Oh no,' I yelled. 'Not that.'

6

I don't know whether or not Star sensed danger. Anyway, he did what horses often do at such times. He lifted up his tail and let a large steaming flow of horse droppings fall on to the road. Then he took a few steps towards Guts and the line of people.

Guts pointed the remote control at us and hit the REWIND button. 'Stop,' I screamed. But it was too late. Star began to go into reverse. She walked a few steps backwards. The pile of horse droppings began to stir. It twisted and lifted. Then it flew through the air – back to where it came from.

The line of people roared. Some laughed. Some screamed. Some ran off. How embarrassing. I was filled with shame. Poor Star went into a backwards trot. Then, suddenly she froze. We all froze. Guts had hit the PAUSE button. He had turned Shaun, Star and me into statues.

While we were standing there like stiff dummies the bus pulled up. All the people in the queue piled on. They couldn't get on quickly enough. They wanted to get away from the mad boys and their even madder horse.

After four or five minutes the pause effect wore off. We were able to move. I climbed down off Star's back. 'Sorry,' I said to Shaun. 'I didn't know that was going to happen.'

Shaun stared down at me. He looked pale. 'I think I've just had a bad dream,' he said. 'In the middle of the day. I think I'd better go home.' He shook his head slowly and then trotted off.

7

'Rats,' I said to myself. Everything was going wrong. I had lost the remote control. Guts Garvey had nicked it and there was nothing I could do about it. I was too scared to go near him in case he put me into reverse again. I felt terrible. I walked home with slow, sad footsteps.

When I got home Dad was mad because the remote control had disappeared. I couldn't tell him what had happened. He would never believe it. I had to spend most of the weekend pretending to help him look for it. The video wouldn't work without the control.

On Monday it was back to school as usual. Back to wandering around with no one to talk to.

As I walked around the schoolyard my stomach rumbled. I was hungry. Very hungry. I hadn't had anything to eat since tea time on Friday night. The reason for this was simple. This was the day of The Great Spaghetti Pig-Out. A competition to see who could eat the most spaghetti bolognese in fifteen minutes.

The grand final was to be held in the school hall. The winner received a free trip to London for two and the entrance money went to charity. I had a good chance of winning. Even though I was skinny I could eat a lot when I was hungry. I had won all the heats. My record was ten bowls of spaghetti bolognese in fifteen minutes. Maybe if I won the competition I would also win the respect of the kids. I was going to give the tickets to London to Mum and Dad. They needed a holiday badly.

I didn't see Guts Garvey until just before the competition. He kept out of my sight all day. I knew he was cooking up some scheme but I didn't know what it was.

There were four of us up on the platform. Me, two girls and Guts Garvey. The hall was packed with kids and teachers. I felt confident but nervous. I knew that I could win. I looked at Guts Garvey and saw that he was grinning his head off. Then I saw Rabbit in the front row. His pocket was bulging. Rabbit had something in his pocket and I thought I knew what it was.

They were up to no good. Guts and Rabbit had something cooked up and it wasn't spaghetti.

The plates of steaming spaghetti bolognese were lined up in front of us. Everything was ready for the starter to say 'go'. My empty stomach was in a knot. My mind was spinning. I tried to figure out what they were up to. What if I ate five plates of spaghetti and Rabbit put me into reverse? I would un-eat it like the man in the cafe. I would go backwards and take all of the spaghetti out and put it back on the plate. My knees started to knock.

I decided to back out of the competition. I couldn't go through with it.

'Go,' yelled Mr Stepney, the school principal. It was too late. I had to go on.

I started shovelling spaghetti into my mouth. There was no time to mix in the meat sauce. I just pushed in the platefuls as they came. One, two, three. The winner would be the one to eat the most plates in fifteen minutes.

I watched Guts and the others out of the corner of my eye. I was already ahead by two bowls. In, out, in, out. Spaghetti, spaghetti, spaghetti. I was up to seven bowls, Guts had eaten only four and the two girls had managed two each. I was going to win. Mum and Dad would be pleased.

Rabbit was watching us from the front row. I noticed Guts nod to him. Rabbit took something out of his pocket. I could see that it was the remote control. He was going to put me on rewind. I was gone.

But no. Rabbit was not pointing the control at me. He pointed it at Guts. What was going on? I soon found out. Guts began eating the spaghetti at enormous speed. Just like a movie on fast forward. His fork went up and down to his mouth so quickly that you could hardly see it. He licked like lightning. He swallowed at top speed. Boy did he go. His arms whirled. The spaghetti flew. Ten, eleven, twelve bowls. Thirteen, fourteen, fifteen. He was plates ahead. I didn't have a chance to catch up to Guts the guzzling gourmet. He fed his face like a whirlwind. It was incredible. Inedible. But it really happened.

Rabbit had put Guts on FAST FORWARD so that

he would eat more plates than me in the fifteen minutes. It wasn't fair. But there was nothing I could do.

The audience cheered and shouted. They thought that Guts was fantastic. No one had ever seen anything like it before. He was up to forty bowls. I had only eaten ten and the two girls six each. The siren blew. Guts was the winner. I was second.

He had eaten forty bowls. No one had ever eaten forty bowls of spaghetti before. Rabbit hit FORWARD on the control and Guts stopped eating. Everyone cheered Guts. I looked at my shoes. I felt ill and it wasn't just from eating ten plates of spaghetti. I swallowed. I had to keep it all down. That was one of the rules – you weren't allowed to be sick. If you threw up you lost the competition.

8

Guts stood up. He looked a bit funny. His face was a green colour. His stomach swelled out over his belt. He started to sway from side to side. Then he opened his mouth.

Out it came. A great tumbling, surge of spew. A tidal wave of swallowed spaghetti and meat sauce. It flowed down the table and on to the floor. A brown and white lake of sick. Guts staggered and tottered. He lurched to the edge of the stage. He opened his mouth again and let forth another avalanche. The kids in the front row screamed as the putrid waterfall splashed down. All over Rabbit.

Rabbit shrieked and sent the remote control spinning into the air. I jumped forward and grabbed it.

I shouldn't have done what I did. But I couldn't help myself. I pointed the control at Guts and the river of sick.

Then I pressed REWIND.

9

After that Guts Garvey was not very popular at school. To say the least. But I had lots of friends. And Mum and Dad had a great time in London.

And as to what happened to the remote control … Well. That's another story.

Nails

Lehman's father sat still on his cane chair. Too still.

A hot breeze ruffled his hair. He stared out of the window at the island. But he did not see. He did not move. He did not know that Lehman was alone.

But the boy knew. He realized he was trapped. Their boat had sunk in the storm. And their radio had gone with it. There was not another soul for a thousand miles. Lehman was rich. The house was his now. The whole island belonged to him. The golden beach. The high hill. The palms. And the little pier where their boat had once bobbed and rocked.

He had no more tears. He had cried them all. Every one. He wanted to rush over and hug his father back to life. He wanted to see that twisted grin again. 'Dad, Dad,' he called.

But the dead man had no reply for his son.

Lehman knew that he had to do something. He

had to close his father's eyes. That was the first thing. But he couldn't bring himself to do it. What if they wouldn't move? What if they were brittle? Or cold? Or soggy?

And then what? He couldn't leave his father there. Sitting, stiff and silent in the terrible heat. He had to bury him. Where? How? He knew that no one would come. The blue sea was endless. Unbroken. Unfriendly to a boy on his own.

Lehman started to scratch nervously. His nails were growing. More of them all the time.

He decided to do nothing for a bit longer. He sat and sat and sat. And remembered how it was when they had come to the island. Just the two of them.

2

'Is that where we live?' said Lehman.

They both looked at the tumbledown hut on top of the hill. 'We'll fix it up in no time,' said Dad. 'It'll soon be like it was in the old days. When I first came here. As good as new.'

And after a while it was. It was home. Lehman became used to it. Even though he was lonely. Every morning he did his school work. Dad told him which books to read. And how to do his sums. Then he left Lehman alone with his studies. And disappeared along the beach.

Dad searched the shore. But he never let Lehman go with him. He took his camera and his knapsack. And his shovel. He peered out into the endless sea. He dug in the golden sand. And every lunch time he returned with rocks and strange objects from the sea.

'One day I'll hit the jackpot,' he said for the thousandth time. 'Maybe tomorrow. Tomorrow I'll find one. Tomorrow will be the day. You'll see.' Then he grew sad. 'There were plenty here once.' He dumped his sack in the corner. It thumped heavily on the floor.

'Let's see what you've got,' said Lehman.

Dad shook his head. 'When I find what I'm looking for you'll be the first to know.' He picked up the sack and took it into his room. He shut the door with a smile.

Lehman knew what his father was doing. He was putting his finds into the old box. The sea chest with the heavy brass lock. Lehman longed to take a look. He wanted to know what his father was searching for. But it was a secret.

He began to scratch his fingers. Just as Dad came out of his room. 'I've told you not to do that,' said Dad.

'I'm itchy,' said Lehman. 'On the fingers. And the toes.'

'Eczema,' Dad told him. 'I used to get it when I was a boy. It'll go when the wind changes.' But he didn't look too sure. He examined the red lumps growing behind Lehman's fingernails. Then he stamped out of the hut.

3

Lehman stared around the silent bungalow. He was lonely. Dad was good company. But he was a man. Lehman wanted friends. And his mother. He picked up her photograph. A lovely, sad face. Staring at him from the oval frame. 'Where did you go?' whispered Lehman. 'I can't even remember you.'

The face seemed to say that it knew. Understood. But it was only a photo of a woman's head. A woman lost in the past. In her hair she wore a golden clip set with pearls.

During the day, Lehman kept the photo on the kitchen table where he worked. And at night he placed it on his bedside table. It watched over him while he slept.

Lehman sighed and closed his book. He looked up as Dad came back carrying some potatoes from their vegetable patch. 'I'm going early in the morning,' he said. 'Just go on with the work I set you today. I'll be back at lunch time.'

'Let me come with you,' pleaded Lehman.

His father looked at him in silence. Then he said, 'When I find what I'm looking for. Then I'll take you.'

'It's not fair,' shouted Lehman. 'I'm all alone here. Every morning. You owe it to me to tell me what you're looking for. I don't even know what we're doing here.'

'I can't tell you,' said Dad slowly. 'Not yet. Trust me.'

That night, in bed, Lehman's eczema was worse. He scratched his itching fingers and toes until they hurt. He dreamed of dark places. And watery figures. Faces laughing. And calling. Voices seemed to whisper secrets from inside his father's sea chest.

In the morning he stared at his itching fingers. And gasped. At first he couldn't take it in. He had ten fingernails. On each hand. Another row of nails had grown behind the first ones. Clean, pink, little fingernails.

He tore back the sheets and looked at his toes. The same thing had happened. A second row of toenails had burst out of the skin. They pointed forwards. Lapping slightly over the first row.

'Dad,' he screamed. 'Dad, Dad, Dad. Look. Something's wrong with me. My nails. I've got too many nai …!' His voice trailed off. He remembered. Dad was down at the beach. On another secret search.

4

Lehman had been told never to go down the path to the cove. Dad had told him it was dangerous. And out of bounds.

But this was an emergency. Lehman stared in horror at his hands. He pulled at one of the new nails. It hurt when he tugged. It was real. It was there to stay. He staggered as he ran down the steep track to the beach. Tears of fright and anger streamed down his cheeks. His chest hurt. His breath tore harshly at his throat.

He pounded on to the hot sand and stared along the shore. His father was nowhere to be seen. Lehman took a guess and ran along the beach to his right. He came to a group of large rocks that blocked his way. The only way around was through the water. He waded into the gently lapping waves. The water came up to his armpits. He carefully strode on, feeling gently with his feet for rocky holes.

At the deepest point the water came up to his chin. But he was nearly round the corner now. Lehman let his feet leave the bottom. He began to swim. He rounded the rocks and splashed into a small cove that he had never seen before.

His father was digging in the pebbles against a rocky wall. At first he didn't see Lehman. Then he looked up. And noticed the dripping figure staggering out of the waves. His face broke into a radiant smile. The look of someone who has found a pot of gold. Then he saw that it was Lehman and his face grew angry.

'I told you never to come here,' he shouted. 'I can't believe that you'd spy on me. You'll ruin everything. Go back. Go back.' He wasn't just cross. He was furious.

Lehman said nothing. He just held out his hands. Turned the backs of his fingers towards his father. There was a long silence. His father's anger melted.

He stared at the double row of nails. Silently Lehman pointed to his feet. They both gazed down.

'Oh no,' said Dad. 'No. I never expected this. Not really.'

'What is it?' yelled Lehman. 'Am I going to die?'

'No. You're not going to die.'

'I need a doctor,' said Lehman.

'No,' said Dad. 'A doctor can't do anything. Not for that.'

'What is it? What's wrong with me? You have to tell me.' They stared at each other. Both afraid.

Dad sat down on a rock. 'I can't tell you. Not yet. What I'm looking for here. It's got something to do with it. If I find what I'm looking for it will be all right. You won't have to worry. But I can't tell. Not yet.'

'What if you never find it?' said Lehman.

'I will,' said Dad. 'I have to.'

Lehman scratched the back of his hands and up his arms. The itch was growing worse. And spreading.

Dad looked around as if he was frightened of Lehman seeing something. As though he had a guilty secret. 'Go home,' he said. 'I'll pack my things and follow. We'll talk back at the house.'

5

Lehman pushed into the water. His mind swirled. His arms itched. Something was terribly wrong. He turned around and shouted back, 'What's going on? You're not telling. I've got a right to know.'

Tears pricked his eyes. Tears of anger and frustration. Dad hung his head. 'Go back,' he called. 'We'll talk. But not here.'

Lehman swam out into the swell. He passed the furthest rock and headed back to the beach on the other side. Dad was out of sight now. Lehman's feet touched the bottom and he walked through the water past a deep, black cave in the rocks.

Something moved inside.

The world froze. Lehman could hear the blood pumping in his head. A shiver spread over his skin like a wave. He choked off a cry. Two dark eyes stared out at him. He turned and thrashed through the water. Half swimming. Half running. Falling. Splashing in panic. He fell and sank under the surface. When he came up he snatched a frightened glance back at the black space between the rocks. He caught a glimpse of a man's face. Staring. Watching. Hiding.

Lehman fled along the beach, stumbling in terror,

not daring to look behind him. He didn't stop until he reached the bungalow. He rushed inside. The thin walls and open windows offered no protection. But he felt better. His breath slowed. His heart beat less loudly. He looked back down the track and wondered if Dad was safe.

He scratched his elbows. And then screamed. More nails had grown. Rows and rows of them. Along his fingers and the backs of his hands. And up over his wrists.

Perfectly formed fingernails lapped over each other. They looked like two gloves of armour.

The world around began to spin. Lehman felt dizzy. His legs wobbled. He looked down. The backs of his toes, feet and ankles were covered too. A gleaming pair of toenail socks grew out of his skin. He opened his mouth to call out. And then fainted on to the floor.

6

When he awoke, the first thing Lehman saw was the photo of his mother. Her soft smile seemed to have faded. The pearl clip in her hair was dull. Then he realized that his eyes were half closed. He was staring at the world through his eyelashes. He suddenly remembered the nails. Was it a dream? He sat up and found himself on his bed. He stared at his hands. The nails had grown up his arms to his elbows. His legs were covered too. Toenails grew up to his knees.

Dad put out a hand and gently touched his shoulder. 'It's OK,' he said. 'Everything is going to be all right. Don't worry.'

Lehman smiled for a second. Dad was safe. Then he examined the nails. The smile disappeared. He was angry.

'Don't worry,' he yelled. 'Don't worry. Look at my arms. And legs. I'm covered in nails. I'm not normal. What are we doing here? What are you looking for down on the beach?' He stared at the photo next to his bed. 'What happened to my mother? I want to know what's going on.'

The wind rattled the windows and shook the bungalow. A sultry storm was brewing up. Far down below their boat tugged and pulled at the ropes that tied it to the pier.

Dad took a deep breath. 'OK,' he said. 'It's time I told you everything.' He stood up and shut the shaking window. He raised his voice above the noise of the wind. 'I don't know where to start,' he said.

Lehman held up a nail-covered arm. 'Start here,' he cried. 'What's happening to me?' As they looked, another row of nails slowly erupted from his left arm, just above the elbow. It was like watching a flower open in fast forward. Lehman felt nothing. It wasn't painful.

Dad stroked the nails gently. As if Lehman was a cat. 'You're not sick,' he said. 'But I think more nails will grow.'

'How many more nails? Will they grow on my face? On my head? On my chest?'

Dad gave a kindly smile. 'Not your face. Maybe the rest of you though. I can't be sure. But I can find out. That's what I'm here for.'

7

There was a long silence. 'Are you looking for that man?' said Lehman.

'What man?' snapped Dad. His eyes were startled.

'I saw a face in the rocks. Down by the point. He was staring at me. Spying.'

'What did he look like?' said Dad. His voice was shrill and urgent.

'I don't know. I was scared. I only saw his eyes. I ran off.'

'This is it,' yelped Dad. 'This is what I've been waiting for. This is the answer to the problem.' He hurried off to the window and looked down at the sea. The waves were crashing now. The wind whipped at them, tearing off their foamy tops and pelting them into the humid skies.

'I'm going,' said Dad. 'Wait here. Wait here. Everything will be all right.'

'No way,' said Lehman. 'You're not leaving me behind again. I'm coming too.'

Shutters banged and a blast of wind broke into the hut like a violent burglar. Everything shook.

'There's going to be a terrible storm,' yelled Dad. 'You can't come, it's too dangerous.'

'If you go – I go,' said Lehman. He looked his father straight in the eye. They stared at each other.

'This is a once-in-a-lifetime chance,' said Dad. 'He might go. I have to ...'

'What's it got to do with this?' yelled Lehman. He held up his arms. The nails had crept up to his shoulders. And another row was growing. Budding like an ivory chain around his neck. 'What about me? It's all right for you. Look at your skin. Normal. Look at me. Covered in nails. Don't you care?'

'It's because I care,' said Dad. He had tears in his eyes. He tried to explain. 'When we were here before. When you were young …'

'I don't remember,' said Lehman. 'You know I don't.'

'No,' said Dad. 'But you were here. And your mother. And that man. He might. He's our only chance to …'

A terrible gust of wind shook the bungalow. Thunder rumbled in the distance. The sky was torn and savage. Dad stared outside. His face was as wild as the storm. 'I have to go,' he said. 'Later. I'll explain later.' He ran to the door and vanished into the lashing wind.

8

Lehman followed his father, still dressed in nothing but shorts. He didn't feel the raging wind. Or the stinging rain. He didn't notice the nails still growing and spreading. A worse fear had filled him. He was frightened for his father. Lehman couldn't see him but he knew that he was somewhere ahead. Down the track that led to the beach.

The wind screamed and howled. Tore at his hair. Stung his eyes. He hurried on and finally found his father. He was standing at the end of the track. Staring into the furious waves which dashed up the beach and crashed into the cliff. The rocks in which the stranger had hidden were nearly covered. They were cut off by the surf. There was no safe way to get to them.

Dad peered at the sand which was revealed as the sea sucked back each wave. He measured the distance to the rocks with his eyes. Then he turned and shouted over the noise of the wind. 'Is that where he was? Is that where you saw the man?'

Lehman nodded and then grabbed his father's arm. 'Don't go,' he yelled. 'It's too rough. You won't have a chance.'

Dad snatched away his arm. He waited as a large wave began its sweep back from the beach. He jumped and ran along the sodden sand. His feet made deep, wet footprints which filled with water. The wave raced back into the sea, leaving the beach clear. A new wave ate the old and began its forward rush.

The desperate man was half way. He sank up to his ankles with each step. The wet sand slowed him to a stumbling crawl. 'Go,' whispered Lehman. 'Go, go, go.' He watched the approaching wave grow. 'Don't,' he said. 'Don't.'

The wave took no notice. It raced hungrily up the beach. It swirled around Dad's ankles. Knocked him from his feet. Buried him in its angry foam.

9

Lehman squinted and peered into the water. His father was gone. The waves were empty. Then he saw a helpless bundle washing out into the deep. Dad raised an arm. And then another. He was swimming far out. His arms flayed. He seemed to be moving into deeper water. He was helpless against the strength of the sea. 'I'm coming,' yelled Lehman. He stepped forward, waiting for the next backwash.

But before he could move, he noticed Dad riding the crest of a wave. Surfing inwards at enormous speed. A tiny, helpless cork rushing forward towards the waiting cliff.

Lehman sighed with relief. And then fright. The wave was too big. It was going to run up to the cliff and kill itself on the rocks. It seemed to gather all its strength. It flung Dad full into the jagged boulders.

And then left him, hanging helplessly on a small ledge.

Without another thought, Lehman jumped on to the sand. He had to get to Dad before the next wave began its run. He made it just in time. He grabbed the stunned man by his shirt and dragged him to his feet. Dad stumbled and leaned on Lehman as the next wave crashed around them.

It sucked and pulled at their legs. Tried to topple them. But Lehman felt a strange strength. It was almost as if the sea had no power over him. He dragged his father back to the steps where they sat sodden and panting. The disappointed waves swirled and smashed below them.

Dad tried to stand. He took a few steps like a drunken man. Lehman noticed a huge swelling on his father's head. A lump as big as a tennis ball. His eyes swivelled and he started to fall.

Lehman grabbed his father by the arm. He managed to drag him, stumbling up to the house. It took all his strength. His sides ached. His chest throbbed with pain. He burst through the door and dumped his father into the chair.

Dad stared out of the window. His eyes were glazed. As the wind dropped and the storm grew still, he held out a shaking arm. He pointed down to the beach. Then he drew a deep breath, shuddered, and was still.

Lehman knew that his father was dead. Silent tears trickled down his cheeks and splashed on the nails that covered his chest. He sat there like a sorrowful knight of old. A warrior in a coat of mail. Crying for a friend who had fallen.

10

All night Lehman sat. And all morning. He'd never seen a dead person before. He didn't know what to do. Finally he stood up and walked to the door. He looked out at the sea. He wanted help. But he didn't want anyone to come.

He knew he could never leave the island. Not while he was covered in nails. He couldn't go back to the world. A world that would laugh. Or stare and wonder. He could see himself sitting in a school desk. Raising an encrusted arm.

He walked back into the room and looked at Dad. He had to do it now. Or he never would. He gently closed his father's eyes. They were soft but cold. It was like shutting a book at the end of a story. A book which would never be opened again. But a book which would never be forgotten. Not for as long as the waves beat on the lonely beach below.

Dad would be heavy. Lehman knew that. He had to dig a grave close to the house.

He chose a sandy spot that overlooked the sea. Lehman could just see the rocks jutting out where he had seen the face. He started to talk to his father as if he were still there. Standing by him.

'This is the place,' he said. 'You can see down there. Maybe what you wanted will come. Whatever it was.'

The sand was soft. He dug easily and soon had a shallow trench hollowed in the sand. It came up to his knees. He didn't want to make it too deep. Not because the work was hard. But because he couldn't bear to drop his father into a gaping hole. Something might bump. Or break.

Lehman returned to the silent man. He grabbed his father under the arms and tugged him slowly out of the door. The dead weight was heavy. Dad's feet dragged and bumped down the steps.

Lehman lowered him gently into the grave.

He looked down at the silent figure, stretched out. It was as if he was sleeping peacefully in the sand. Lehman picked up the shovel. But something was wrong. He felt bad. As if he had to do something that would hurt. Then he knew what it was. He couldn't put a shovelful of sand on his father's face. Even though he was dead.

He fetched an old newspaper from inside. Then he looked at the gentle face for the last time and covered it with the paper. He filled the hole with sand and smoothed it down. He had no strength left to make a gravestone so he pushed the shovel into the sand. And left it standing as a tall marker.

'Goodbye, Dad,' he said.

Lehman stood and stared out to sea. The sun glinted on the thousands of nails that covered almost every part of him. He looked like a tall lizard man. Standing. Waiting. Daring an invader to come.

There was no boat on the water. He didn't care. He didn't want anyone to see him as he was, covered in nails. A great feeling of loneliness filled him. As far as he knew, there was no one else in the world like him.

11

He walked inside and looked in the mirror. His face was clear. But his chest, back, arms and legs were covered in the new nails. He suddenly opened a drawer. And pulled out some nail clippers. He wondered if he would have to spend his life clipping thousands of nails as they grew. He laughed wildly and threw the clippers out of the open window.

It had taken him all afternoon to dig the grave.

The sun was beginning to sink lower in the sky. In an hour or two it would be dark. And he was alone. He wondered if he should lock the windows. And bolt the door. He knew that tonight – when the dark came – he would be frightened.

The face in the cave would come. Creeping. Stealing up the path. Wandering in the shadows. He knew that he would jump at every sound. He would try not to sleep. But in the end sleep would come. And so would the unknown man.

He jumped to his feet. 'You won't get me,' he shouted. 'I'll get you.'

He ran outside and sharpened a long stick with the axe. Now he had a spear. He marched down the path towards the beach. His legs felt weak. His stomach was cold and heavy. He wanted to turn. And run. And hide.

But he forced himself on until he reached the beach. The sea was still and blue. It lapped gently on the sandy beach. The wild waves had gone. Lehman strode along the sand towards the rocks. And the cave.

He shuddered even though the air was warm. He gripped the spear tightly with his nailed fingers. The tide was out and the small cave now opened on to the sand. He reached the entrance and peered into the gloom.

There were soft, dripping noises. And the sound of steady breathing. Someone was in there.

'Come out,' he shrieked. His voice cracked and ended in a squeak. He coughed and tried again. 'Come out, whoever you are.' The words echoed in the cave. Then something moved. He thought he heard a slippery, rustling noise.

His courage fled. He started walking backwards, too frightened to turn around.

12

Three people came out of the cave. If people is the word. Two men. And a smaller one. They wore no clothes. But instead, were covered from neck to toe – in nails.

Lehman felt faint. He couldn't take it in. He

wondered if this island gave people the terrible nail disease.

They smiled at him. Warm, friendly smiles. The child giggled nervously. The nail people were wet. They had been in the sea. Water glistened and sparkled from their nails. They shone like neat rows of wet glass.

One of the men pointed into the deep water further out. A swift shadow like a shark circling moved far down. It rushed towards the shore with the speed of a train. Then burst out of the water and back in again.

Lehman caught a glimpse of a sparkling fish tail. And fair hair. It swirled several times. And then climbed on to a rock. A woman with long golden hair. And a fish tail covered in nails.

The men laughed. Their chuckles sounded like bubbles bursting out of the water. Lehman stared at the nails which shivered as they moved. He spoke aloud. Half to himself. Half to them. 'Not nails,' he said, 'but scales.'

He turned back to the mermaid. In her hair, she wore a golden clip, set with pearls. The same pin that he had seen every day in his mother's photograph.

In that moment Lehman knew that while his father had been a man, his mother was a mermaid.

She beckoned to him, calling him out into the water. Then she dived down under the rippling surface. The mermen nodded at him, pointing out to sea. Like Lehman, they had legs rather than a tail.

Lehman walked. And walked. And walked. The waves closed over his head. He opened his mouth and took a deep breath of water. It passed through his new gills with a fizz of bubbles. His head was filled with lightness. And happiness. He began to swim, deep down, following his mother.

Then, for a second, he remembered something. He burst upwards faster and faster and plunged out of the water like a dolphin. He snatched one last look at the island. And saw, high on a hill, a small mound. A shovel stood pointing to the bright sky above. He knew now why his father had brought him here. A fish-boy could only be happy in one place – the ocean.

Lehman waved goodbye and then plunged down far below the surface. And followed his family out to sea.

Pink Bow Tie

Well, here I am again, sitting outside the Principal's office. And I've only been at the school for two days. Two lots of trouble in two days! Yesterday I got the strap for nothing. Nothing at all.

I see this bloke walking along the street wearing a pink bow tie. It looks like a great pink butterfly attacking his neck. It is the silliest bow tie I have ever seen. 'What are you staring at, lad?' says the bloke. He is in a bad mood.

'Your bow tie,' I tell him. 'It is ridiculous. It looks like a pink vampire.' It is so funny that I start to laugh my head off.

Nobody tells me that this bloke is Old Splodge, the Principal of the school. He doesn't see the joke and he gives me the strap. Life is very unfair.

Now I am in trouble again. I am sitting here outside Old Splodge's office waiting for him to call me in.

Well, at least I've got something good to look at. Old Splodge's secretary is sitting there typing some letters. She is called Miss Newham and she is a real knockout. Every boy in the school is in love with her. I wish she was my girlfriend, but as she is seventeen and I am only fourteen there is not much hope. Still, she doesn't have a boyfriend so there is always a chance.

She is looking at me and smiling. I can feel my face going red. 'Why have you dyed your hair blond?' she asks sweetly. 'Didn't you know it is against the school rules for boys to dye their hair?'

I try to think of a very impressive answer but before I can say anything Old Splodge sticks his head around the office door. 'Come in, boy,' he says.

I go in and sit down. 'Well, lad,' says Old Splodge. 'Why have you dyed your hair? Trying to be a surfie, eh?' He is a grumpy old boy. He is due to retire next year and he does not want to go.

I notice that he is still wearing the pink bow tie. He always wears this bow tie. He cannot seem to live without it. I try not to look at it as I answer him. 'I did not dye my hair, sir,' I say.

'Yesterday,' says Splodge, 'when I gave you six of

the best, I noticed that you had black hair. Am I correct?'

'Yes, sir,' I answer.

'Then tell me, lad,' he says, 'how is it that your hair is white today?' I notice that little purple veins are standing out on his bald head. This is a bad sign.

'It's a long story,' I tell him.

'Tell me the long story,' he says. 'And it had better be good.'

I look him straight in the eye and this is what I tell him.

2

I am a very nervous person. Very sensitive. I get scared easily. I am scared of the dark. I am scared of ghost stories. I am even scared of the Cookie Monster on *Sesame Street*. Yesterday I am going home on the train after getting the strap and I am in a carriage with some very strange people. There is an old lady with a walking stick, grey hair and gold wire-rim glasses. She is bent right over and can hardly walk. There is also a mean, skinny-looking guy sitting next to me. He looks like he would slit your throat for two bob. Next to him is a kid of about my age and he is smoking. You are not allowed to smoke when you are fourteen. This is why I am not smoking at the time.

After about five minutes a ticket collector puts his head in the door. He looks straight at the kid who is smoking. 'Put that cigarette out,' he says. 'You are too young to smoke.'

The kid does not stop smoking. He picks up this thing that looks like a transistor and twiddles a knob. Then he starts to grow older in front of our eyes. He just slowly changes until he looks about twenty-five. 'How's that?' he says to the ticket collector. 'Am I old enough now?'

The ticket collector gives an almighty scream and runs down the corridor as fast as his legs can take him. The rest of us just sit there looking at the kid (who is now a man) with our mouths hanging open.

'How did you do that?' trembles the old lady. She is very interested indeed.

'Easy,' says the kid-man as he stands up. The train is stopping at a station. 'Here,' he says throwing the transistor thing on to her lap. 'You can have it if you want.' He goes out of the compartment, down the corridor and gets off the train.

We all stare at the box-looking thing. It has a

54

sliding knob on it. Along the right-hand side it says OLDER and at the left end it says YOUNGER. On the top is a label saying AGE RAGER.

The mean-looking bloke sitting next to me makes a sudden lunge forward and tries to grab the Age Rager but the old lady is too quick for him. 'No you don't,' she says and shoves him off. Quick as a flash she pushes the knob a couple of centimetres down towards the YOUNGER end.

Straight away she starts to grow younger. In about one minute she looks as if she is sixteen. She *is* sixteen. She looks kind of pretty in the old lady's glasses and old-fashioned clobber. It makes her look like a hippy. 'Whacko,' she shouts, throwing off her shawl. She throws the Age Rager over to me, runs down the corridor and jumps off the train just as it is pulling out of the station.

As the train speeds past I hear her say, 'John McEnroe, look out!'

'Give that to me,' says the mean-looking guy. Like I told you before, I am no hero. I am scared of my own shadow. I do not like violence or scary things so I hand over the Age Rager to Mean Face.

He grabs the Age Rager from me and pushes the knob nearly up to the end where it says YOUNGER.

Straight away he starts to grow younger but he does not stop at sixteen. In no time at all there is a baby sitting next to me in a puddle of adult clothes. He is only about one year old. He looks at me with a wicked smile. He sure is a mean-looking baby. 'Bad Dad Dad,' he says.

'I am not your Dad Dad,' I say. 'Give me that before you hurt yourself.' The baby shakes his head and puts the Age Rager behind his back. I can see that he is not going to hand it over. He thinks it is a toy.

Then, before I can move, he pushes the knob right up to the OLDER end. A terrible sight meets my eyes. He starts to get older and older. First he is about sixteen, then thirty, then sixty, then eighty, then one hundred and then he is dead. But it does not stop there. His body starts to rot away until all that is left is a skeleton.

I give a terrible scream and run to the door but I cannot get out because it is jammed. I kick and shout but I cannot get out. I open the window but the train is going too fast for me to escape.

And that is how my hair gets white. I have to sit in that carriage with a dead skeleton for fifteen minutes. I am terrified. I am shaking with fear. It is the most horrible thing that has ever happened to me. My hair goes white in just fifteen minutes. I am frightened into being a blond. When the train stops I get out of the window and walk all the rest of the way home.

'And that,' I say to Splodge, 'is the truth.'

3

Splodge is fiddling with his pink bow tie. His face is turning the same colour. I can see that he is about to freak out. 'What utter rubbish,' he yells. 'Do you take me for a fool? Do you expect me to believe that yarn?'

'I can prove it,' I say. I get the Age Rager out of my bag and put it on his desk.

Splodge picks it up and looks at it carefully. 'You can go now, lad,' he says in a funny voice. 'I will send a letter home to your parents telling them that you are suspended from school for telling lies.'

I walk sadly back to class. My parents will kill me if I am suspended from school.

For the next two weeks I worry about the letter showing up in the letter box. But nothing happens. I am saved.

Well, it is not quite true that nothing happens.

Two things happen: one good and one bad. The good thing is that Splodge disappears and is never seen again.

The bad thing is that Miss Newham gets a boyfriend. He is about eighteen and is good-looking.

It is funny though. Why would she go out with a kid who wears pink bow ties?

Ice Maiden

I just wouldn't go anywhere near a redhead.

Now don't get me wrong and start calling me a hairist or something like that. Listen to what I have to say, then make up your mind.

It all started with Mr Mantolini and his sculptures.

They were terrific, were Mr Mantolini's frozen statues. He carved them out of ice and stood them in the window of his fish shop which was over the road from the pier. A new ice carving every month.

Sometimes it would be a beautiful peacock with its tail fanned out. Or maybe a giant fish thrashing itself to death on the end of a line. One of my favourites was a kangaroo with a little joey peering out of her pouch.

It was a bit sad really. On the first day of every month Mr Mantolini would throw the old statue out the back into an alley. Where it would melt and trickle away into a damp patch on the ground.

A new statue would be in the shop window. Sparkling blue and silver as if it had been carved from a solid chunk of the Antarctic shelf.

Every morning on my way to school, I would stop to stare at his statue. And on the first of the month I would be there after school to see the new one. I couldn't bear to go around the back and watch yesterday's sculpture melt into the mud.

'Why do you throw them out?' I asked one day.

Mr Mantolini shrugged. 'You live. You die,' he said.

Mr Mantolini took a deep breath. Now he was going to ask me something. The same old thing he had asked every day for weeks. 'My cousin Tony come from Italy. Next month. You take to school. You friend. My cousin have red hair. You like?'

I gave him my usual answer. 'Sorry,' I said. 'I won't be able to.' I couldn't tell him that it was because I hated red hair. I didn't want to hurt his feelings.

He just stood there without saying anything. He was disappointed in me because we were friends. He knew how much I liked his ice statues and he always came out to talk to me about them. 'You funny boy,' he said. He shook his head and walked inside.

I thought I saw tears in Mr Mantolini's eyes. I knew I had done the wrong thing again. And I was sorry. But I didn't want a redhead for a mate.

2

I felt guilty and miserable all day. But after school I cheered up a bit. It was the first of September. There would be a new ice statue in the window. It was always something to look forward to.

I hurried up to the fish shop and stared through the glass. I couldn't believe what I saw. The ice statue of a girl. It reminded me of one of those Greek sculptures that you see in museums. It had long tangled hair. And smiling lips. Its eyes sparkled like frozen diamonds. I tell you this. That ice girl was something else. She was fantastic.

'You're beautiful,' I said under my breath. 'Beautiful.'

Of course she was only a statue. She couldn't see or hear me. She was just a life-sized ice maiden, standing among the dead fish in the shop window. She was inside a glass fridge which kept her cold. Her cheeks were covered with frost.

I stood there for ages just gawking at her. I know it was stupid. I would have died if anyone knew what

I was thinking. How embarrassing. I had a crush on a piece of ice.

Every day after that, I visited the fish shop. I was late for school because of the ice maiden. I filled every spare minute of my time standing outside the window. It was as if I was hypnotized. The ice maiden's smile seemed to be made just for me. Her outstretched hand beckoned. 'Get real,' I said to myself. 'What are you doing here? You fool.' I knew I was mad but something kept drawing me back to the shop.

Mr Mantolini wouldn't meet my gaze. He was cross with me.

I pretended the ice girl was my friend. I told her my secrets. Even though she was made of ice, I had this silly feeling that she understood.

Mr Mantolini saw me watching her. But he didn't come outside. And whenever I went inside to buy fish for Mum, he scurried out the back and sent his assistant to serve me.

3

The days passed. Weeks went by. The ice maiden smiled on and on. She never changed. The boys thought I was nuts standing there gawking at a lump of ice. But she had this power over me – really. Kids started to tease me. 'He's in love,' said a girl called Simone. I copped a lot of teasing at school but still I kept gazing in that window.

As the days went by I grew sadder and sadder. I wanted to take the ice girl home. I wanted to keep her for ever. But once she was out of her glass cage, in the warm air, her smiling face would melt and drip away.

I dreaded the first of October. When Mr Mantolini would take the ice maiden and dump her in the alley. To be destroyed by the warm rays of the sun.

On the last day of September I waited until Mr Mantolini was serving in the shop. 'You can't throw her out,' I yelled. 'She's too lovely. She's real. You mustn't. You can't.' I was nearly going to say, 'I love her,' but that would have been stupid.

Mr Mantolini looked at me and shrugged. 'You live. You die,' he said. 'She ice. She cold. She water.'

I knew it was no good. Tomorrow Mr Mantolini would cast the ice girl out into the alley.

The next day I wagged school. I hid in the alley and waited. The minutes dragged their feet. The hours seemed to crawl. But then, as I knew he would, Mr

Mantolini emerged with the ice maiden. He dumped her down by the rubbish bins. Her last resting place was to be among the rotting fish heads in an empty alley.

Mr Mantolini disappeared back into the shop. I rushed over to my ice maiden. She was still covered in frost and had sticky, frozen skin.

My plan was to take her to the butcher. I would pay him to keep the ice maiden in his freezer where I could visit her every day. I hadn't asked him yet. But he couldn't say no, could he?

The sun was rising in the sky. I had to hurry.

The ice maiden still stooped. Still reached out. She seemed to know that her time had come. 'Don't worry,' I said. 'I'll save you.'

I don't know what came over me. I did something crazy. I bent down and gently kissed her on the mouth.

4

It was a long kiss. The longest kiss ever in the history of the world. My lips stuck to hers. My flesh froze on to the ice. Cold needles of pain numbed my lips. I tried to pull away but I couldn't. The pain made my eyes water. Tears streamed down my face and across the ice maiden's cheeks.

On we kissed. And on. And on. I wanted to pull my mouth away but much as I cared for the ice girl, I didn't want my lips to tear away, leaving bleeding skin as a painful reminder of my madness. There I was, kissing ice lips, unable to move.

I tried to yell for help but I couldn't speak. Muffled grunts came out of my nose. Horrible nasal noises. No one came to help me. The alley echoed with the noise.

I grabbed the ice maiden and lifted her up. She was heavy. Her body was still sticky with frost. My fingers stuck fast. She was my prisoner. And I was hers.

The sun warmed my back. Tears of agony filled my eyes. If I waited there she would melt. I would be free but the ice maiden would be gone. Her lovely nose and chin would drip away to nothing.

But the cold touch of the ice girl was terrible. Her smiling lips burnt my flesh. The tip of my nose was frozen. I ran out of the alley into the street. There was a group of people waiting by a bus-stop near the end of the pier. 'Help, get me unstuck. But don't hurt the ice maiden,' was what I tried to say.

But what came out was, 'Nmn nnmmm nnnn nng ng ng mn nm.'

The people looked at me as if I was crazy. Some of them laughed. They thought I was acting the fool. An idiot pretending to kiss a statue.

I ran over to Mr Mantolini's shop and tried to knock on the window with my foot. I had to balance on one leg, while holding the ice girl in my arms and painfully kissing her at the same time. I fell over with a crunch. Oh agony, oh misery, oh pain. My lips, my fingers, my knees.

There was no sign of Mr Mantolini. He must have been in the back room.

5

What could I do? I looked out to sea. If I jumped into the water it would melt the ice. My lips and fingers would come free. But the ice maiden would melt. 'Let me go,' I whispered in my mind. But she made no answer.

My hands were numb. Cold pins pricked me without mercy. I ran towards the pier. I spoke to my ice maiden again, without words. 'I'm sorry. I'm sorry, sorry, sorry.'

I jogged along the pier. Further and further. My feet drummed in time with my thoughts. 'Sorry, sorry, sorry.'

I stopped and stared down at the waves. Then I closed my eyes and jumped, still clutching the ice-cold girl to my chest. Down, I plunged. For a frozen moment I hung above the ocean. And then, with a gurgle and a groan, I took the ice lady to her doom.

The waves tossed above us. The warm water parted our lips. My fingers slipped from her side. I bobbed up like an empty bottle and saw her floating away. Already her eyes had gone. Her hair was a glassy mat. The smiling maiden smiled no more. She was just a lump of ice melting in the waves.

'No,' I screamed. My mouth filled with salt water and I sank under the sea.

They say that your past life flashes by you when you are drowning. Well, it's true. I re-lived some horrible moments. I remembered the time in a small country school when I was just a little kid. And the only redhead. I saw the school bully Johnson teasing me every day. Once again I sat on the school bench at lunch-time – alone and rejected. Not allowed to hang around with the others. Just because Johnson didn't like red hair. Once again I could hear him calling me 'carrots' and 'ginger'. They were the last thoughts that came to me before the world vanished into salty blackness.

6

But I didn't drown. In a way my hair saved me. It must have been easy for them to spot my curly locks swirling like red seaweed thrown up from the ocean bed.

Mr Mantolini pulled me out. He and his cousin. I could hear him talking even though I was only half conscious. 'You live. But you not die yet.'

I didn't want to open my eyes. I couldn't bear to think about what I had done to the ice maiden. I was alive but she was dead. Gone for ever.

In the end I looked up. I stared at my rescuers. Mr Mantolini and his cousin.

She had red tangled hair. And smiling lips. Her eyes sparkled like frozen diamonds. I tell you this. That girl Tony was something else. She was fantastic.

'You're beautiful,' I said under my breath. 'Beautiful.'

Mr Mantolini's ice statue had been good. But not as good as the real thing. After all, it had only been a copy of his cousin Tony. I smiled up at her. And she smiled back. With a real smile.

I guess that's when I discovered that an ice maiden who is dead is not sad. And a nice maiden who is red, is not bad.

Not bad at all.

There's No Such Thing

Poor Grandad. They had taken him away and locked him up in a home. I knew he would hate it. He loved to be out in his garden digging the veg or arguing with old Mrs Jingle next door. He wouldn't like being locked away from the world.

'I know it's sad,' said Mum. 'But it's the only thing to do. I am afraid that Grandad has a sort of sickness that's in the head. He doesn't think right. He keeps seeing things that aren't there. It sometimes happens to people when they get very old like Grandad.'

I could feel tears springing into my eyes. 'What sort of things?' I shouted. 'I don't believe it. Grandad's all right. I want to see him.'

Mum had tears in her eyes too. She was just as upset as I was. After all, Grandad was her father. 'You can see him on Monday, Chris,' she said. 'The nurse said you can visit Grandad after school.'

On Monday I went to the sanatorium where they kept Grandad. I had to wait for ages in this little room which had hard chairs and smelt of stuff you clean toilets with. The nurse in charge wore a badge which said, 'Sister Gribble'. She had mean eyes. They looked like the slits on money boxes which take things in but never give anything back. She had her hair done up in a tight bun and her shoes were so clean you could see the reflection of her knobbly knees in them.

'Follow me, lad,' said the nurse after ages and ages. She led me down a corridor and into a small room. 'Before you go in,' she said, 'I want you to know one thing. Whenever the old man talks about things that are not really there, you must say, "There's no such thing." You are not to pretend you believe him.'

I didn't know what she was talking about, but I did know one thing – she shouldn't have called Grandad 'the old man'. He had a name just like everyone else.

We went into the room and there was Grandad, slumped in a bed between stiff, white sheets. He was staring listlessly at a fly on the ceiling. He looked unhappy.

As she went out of the room Nurse Gribble looked at Grandad and said, 'None of your nonsense now. Remember, there's no such thing.' She sat on a chair just outside the door.

2

Grandad brightened up when he saw me. A bit of the old twinkle came back into his eyes. 'Ah, Chris,' he said. 'I've been waiting for you. You've got to help me get out of this terrible place. My tomatoes will be dying. I've got to get out.' He looked at the door and whispered. 'She watches me like a hawk. You are my only chance.'

He pulled something out from under the sheets and pushed it into my hands. It was a small camera with a built-in flash. 'Get a photo,' he said, 'and then they will know it's true. They will have to let me out if you get a photo.'

His eyes were wild and flashing. I didn't know what he was talking about. 'Get a photo of what?' I asked.

'The dragon, Chris. The dragon in the drain. I never told you about it before because I didn't want to scare you. But now you are my only hope. Even your mother thinks I have gone potty. She won't believe me that there is a dragon. No one will.'

A voice like broken glass came from the corridor outside. It said: 'There's no such thing as a dragon.' It was Nurse Gribble. She was listening to our conversation.

I didn't know what to think. It was true then. Poor old Grandad was out of his mind. He thought there was such a thing as a dragon. I decided to go along with it. 'Where is the dragon, Grandad?' I whispered.

'In Donovan's Drain,' he said softly, looking at the door as he spoke. 'Behind my back fence. It's a great horrible brute with green teeth and red eyes. It has scales and wings and a cruel, slashing tail. Its breath is foul and stinks of the grave.'

'And you've seen it?' I croaked.

'Seen it, seen it. I've not only seen it, I've fought it. Man and beast, battling it out in the mouth of Donovan's Drain. It tried to get Doo Dah. It eats dogs. And cats. It loves them. Crunches their bones. But I stopped it, I taught it a thing or two.' Grandad jumped out of bed and grabbed a broom out of a cupboard. He started to battle an imaginary dragon, stabbing at it with the broom and then jumping backwards.

He leaped up on to the bed. He was as fit as a lion. 'Try to get Doo Dah, will you? Try to eat my dog? Take that, and that, you smelly fiend.' He lunged at the dragon that wasn't there, brandishing the broom like a spear. He looked like a small, wild pirate trying to stop the enemy from boarding his ship.

Suddenly a cold, crisp voice cut across the room. 'Get back in bed,' it ordered. It was Nurse Gribble. Her mean eyes flashed. 'Stop this nonsense at once,' she snapped at Grandad. 'There is no such thing as a dragon. It's all in your head. You are a silly old man.'

'He's not,' I shouted. 'He's not silly. He's my Grandad and he shouldn't be in here. He wants to get out.'

The nurse narrowed her eyes until they were as thin as needles. 'You are upsetting him,' she said to me. 'I want you out of here in five minutes.' Then she spun around and left the room.

'I've got to escape,' said Grandad as he climbed slowly back into his bed. 'I've got to see the sun and the stars and feel the breeze on my face. I've got to touch trees and smell the salt air at the beach. And my tomato plants – they will die without me. This place is a jail. I would sooner be dead than live here.' His bottom lip started to tremble. 'Get a photo, Chris.

Get a photo of the dragon. Then they will know it's true. Then they will have to let me out. I'm not crazy – there really is a dragon.'

He grabbed my arm and stared urgently into my eyes. 'Please, Chris, please get a photo.'

'OK, Grandad,' I told him. 'I'll get a photo of a dragon, even if I have to go to the end of the earth for it.'

His eyes grew wilder. 'Don't go into the drain. Don't go into the dragon's lair. It's too dangerous. He will munch your bones. Hide. Hide at the opening and when he comes out take his photo. Then run. Run like crazy.'

'When does it come out?'

'At midnight. Always at midnight. That's why you need the flash on the camera.'

'How long since you last saw the dragon, Grandad?' I asked.

'Two years,' he said.

'Two years,' I echoed. 'It might be dead by now.'

'If it is dead,' said Grandad, 'then I am as good as dead too.' He looked gloomily around the sterile room.

I heard an impatient sigh from outside. 'Visiting time is over,' said Nurse Gribble, in icy tones.

I gave Grandad a kiss on his prickly cheek. 'Don't worry,' I whispered in his ear. 'If there is a dragon I will get his photo.' The nurse was just about busting her ear-drums trying to hear what I said but it was too soft for her to make out the words.

As she showed me out, Nurse Gribble spoke to me in her sucked-lemon voice. 'Remember, boy, there's no such thing as a dragon. If you humour the old man you will not be allowed back.'

I shook my head as I walked home. Poor Grandad. He thought there was a dragon in Donovan's Drain. I didn't know what to do now. I didn't believe in dragons but a promise is a promise. I would have to go to Donovan's Drain at midnight at least once. I tried to think of some other way to get Grandad out of that terrible place but nothing came to my mind.

3

And that is how I came to find myself sitting outside the drain in the middle of the night. It was more like a tunnel than a drain. It disappeared into the black earth from which came all manner of smells and noises. I shivered and waited but nothing happened.

No dragon. After a while I walked down to the opening and peered in. I could hear the echo of pinging drips of water and strange gurglings. It was as black as the insides of a rat's gizzards.

In the end I went there five nights in a row. I didn't see Grandad in that time because the nurse would only let me visit once a week. Each night I sat and sat outside the drain but not the slightest trace of a dragon appeared. It gave me time to think and I started to wonder if perhaps Grandad's story could be true. What if he had seen a dragon? It could be asleep for the winter – hibernating. Perhaps dragons slept for years. It might not come out again for ten years. In the end I decided there was only one way to find out.

I had to go in.

The next night I crept out of the back door when Mum was asleep. I carried a torch and Grandad's camera and I wore a parka and two jumpers. It was freezing.

I walked carefully along the drain with one foot on either side of the small, smelly stream that ran down the middle. It was big enough for me to stand upright. I was scared, I will tell you that now. It was absolutely black to the front. Behind me the dull night glow of the entrance grew smaller and smaller. I didn't want to go but I forced myself to keep walking into the blackness. Finally I looked back and could no longer see the entrance.

I was alone in the bowels of the earth in the middle of the night. I remembered Grandad's words. 'Don't go into the dragon's lair. It's too dangerous. He will munch your bones.'

I also remembered Nurse Gribble's words. 'There's no such thing as a dragon.' I almost wished she was right.

The strong beam of the torch was my only consolation. I shone it in every crack and nook. Suddenly the idea of a dragon did not seem silly. In my mind I could see the horrible beast with red eyes and dribbling saliva, waiting there to clasp me in its cruel claws.

I don't know how I did it but I managed to walk on for a couple of hours. I had to try. I had to check out Grandad's tale. I owed him that much.

Finally the tunnel opened into a huge cavern. It was big enough to fit ten houses inside. Five tunnels opened into the cavern. Four of them were made out of concrete but the fifth was more like a cave that had been dug out by a giant rabbit. The earth sides were covered in a putrid green slime and deep scratch marks.

I carefully made my way into the mouth of this cave. I wanted to turn and run. I wanted to scream. I half wished that a dragon would grab me and finish me off just to get it over and done with. Anything would be better than the terror that shook my jellied flesh.

I stumbled and fell many times, as the floor was covered in the same slime as the walls. The tunnel twisted around and upwards like a corkscrew. As I progressed a terrible smell became stronger and stronger. It was so bad that I had to tie my handkerchief over my mouth.

Just as I was about to give up I stood on something that scrunched under my feet. It was a bone. I shone the torch on the floor and saw that small bones were scattered everywhere. There were bones of every shape and size – many of them were small skulls. On one I noticed a circle of leather with a brass tag attached. It said 'Timmy'. I knew it was a dog's collar.

As I pushed on, the bones became deeper and deeper until at last they were like a current sweeping around my knees. My whole body was shaking with fear but still I pressed on. I had to get that photo.

The only way to get Grandad out of that sanatorium was to prove he wasn't mad.

Finally the tunnel opened up into another cavern that was so large my torch beam could not reach the roof. And in the middle, spread out across a mountain of treasure, was the dragon.

4

His cruel white jaws gaped at me and his empty eyes were pools of blackness. He made no movement and neither did I. I stood there with my knees banging together like jackhammers.

The horrible creature did not jump up and crunch my bones. He couldn't. He was dead.

He was just a pile of bones with his wings stretched out in one last effort to protect his treasure. He had been huge and ugly. The dried-out bones of his wings were petrified in earthbound flight. His skull dripped with slime and leered at me as if he still sought to snap my tiny body in two.

And the treasure that he sought to hoard? It was poor indeed. Piles of junk. Broken television sets, discarded transistor radios, dustbin lids, old car wheels, bottles, a broken pram, cracked mirrors and twisted picture frames. There was not a diamond or a gold sword to be seen. The dragon had been king of a junk heap. He had saved every piece of rubbish that had floated down the drain.

Now I could get what I came for. I could take a photo. I stood on a smooth rock and snapped away with my camera. This was the evidence that would save Grandad. I took about ten photos before my foot slipped and the torch and camera spun into the air. I heard them clatter on to the dragon's pile of junk. The torch blinked as it landed and then flicked out. I was in pitch blackness. Alone with a dead dragon.

I felt my way carefully forward trying to find the camera. The rock on which I had stood was not a rock at all. It was a smooth type of box with rounded corners. I felt it carefully with my fingers, then I started to grope my way forward. I had to find the camera and the torch but in my heart I knew that it was impossible. They were somewhere among the dragon's junk. Somewhere under his rotting bones. I knew I would never find either of them in the dark.

As I started to grope around in the rubbish I bumped into an old oil drum. It clattered down the heap making a terrible clacking as it went.

Suddenly I felt the damp ground tremble. The noise had loosened the roof of the cave. Pieces of rock and stone started to fall from above. The cave was collapsing. The earth shook as huge boulders fell from the roof above. I had to get out before I was buried alive. I stumbled back through the rubbish to the tunnel and fought my way through the piles of bones. I often hit my head on a rock or slipped on the slimy floor. I could hear an enormous crashing and squelching coming from behind. Suddenly a roaring filled the air and a blast of air sent me skidding down the corkscrew passage. The whole roof of the cavern must have fallen in.

I skidded down the slippery tube on my backside. The floor was rough and the seat was ripped out of my pants as I tumbled down and down.

At last I landed upside down at the bottom. I was aching all over and although I couldn't see anything I knew I must be bleeding.

A bouncing noise was coming from above. Something was tumbling down after me. Before I could move, a hard, rubbery object crashed into me and knocked me down. It was the smooth box-thing that I had stood on.

I just sat there in the gurgling water and cried. It

had all been in vain. I had seen the remains of the dragon and taken the photo. But the camera and the dragon and his rubbishy treasure were all buried under tonnes of rock. The dragon was gone for ever and so was Grandad's hope of getting out of the sanatorium. There was no proof that the dragon had ever lived.

5

I could feel the box-thing move off down the drain. It was floating. I decided to follow it downstream and I think that it probably saved my life. By following the floating cube I was able to find my way back without a torch.

At last – wet, cold and miserable – I emerged into the early morning daylight. The whole adventure had been for nothing. Everyone would still think that Grandad was crazy and I was the only one who knew he wasn't. All I had to show for my efforts was the rubbery cube. I had no proof that a dragon had once lived in the drain.

I looked at the cube carefully. It looked like a huge dice out of a game of Trivial Pursuit except it had no spots on it. It was heavy and coloured red. I could see it had no lid. It was solid, not hollow. I decided to show it to Grandad.

I carried the cube back home and had a shower. Mum had gone to work. I got into some clean clothes and went round to the sanatorium. The mean-eyed nurse sat in her glass prison warder's box at the end of the corridor.

'Well,' she said sarcastically, 'where is your dragon photo?'

'I haven't got one,' I said sadly, 'but I have got this.' I held up the cube.

'What is it?' she snapped.

'It's from the dragon's cave,' I said weakly.

'You nasty little boy,' she replied. 'Don't think your lies are going to get the old man out. You make sure that when you leave that smelly box leaves too.'

I went down to Grandad's room. His face lit up when he saw me but it soon grew sad as he listened to my story.

'I'm finished, Chris,' he said. 'Now I will never be able to prove my story. I'm stuck here for life.'

We both sat and stared miserably at the cube. Suddenly Grandad sat up in bed. 'Wait a minute,' he said. 'I've read about something like that in a book.'

He pointed at the cube. 'I think I know what it is.'
He was smiling.

As he spoke, I noticed a crack appearing up one
side. With a sudden snap the whole thing broke in
half and a little dragon jumped out.

'It's a dragon's egg,' shouted Grandad. 'Dragon's
eggs are cube shaped.'

The little monster ran straight at my leg, snapping
its teeth. It was hungry. I jumped up on the bed with
Grandad and we both laughed. Its teeth were sharp.

The dragon was purple with green teeth. Smoke
was coming out of its ears.

'I'm getting out of here,' said Grandad. 'They can't
keep me now. We can prove I saw a dragon in the
drain. This little fellow didn't come from nowhere.
I'm free at last.'

'Hooray,' I shouted at the top of my voice. 'It really
is a dragon.'

Just then I heard the clip, clop sound of Nurse
Gribble's shoes. The little dragon stood still and
sniffed. He was looking at the door. He could smell
food.

Nurse Gribble stepped into the room and started
to speak. 'There's no such thing …' Her voice turned
into a shriek as the tiny new-born dragon galloped

across the room and clamped its teeth on to her leg. 'Help,' she screamed. 'Help, help. Get it off. Get it off. A horrible little dragon. It's biting me.' She hopped from one side of the room to the other with the dragon clinging on to her leg tightly with its teeth. She yelled and screamed and jumped but the dragon would not let go.

Grandad headed for the door carrying his suitcase.

Nurse Gribble started to shriek, 'Don't go, don't go. Don't leave me alone with this dragon.'

Grandad looked at her. 'Don't be silly,' he said. 'There's no such thing as a dragon.'

Only Gilt

The bird's perch is swinging to and fro and hitting me on the nose. I can see my eye in its little mirror. Its water dish is sliding around near my chin. The smell of old bird droppings is awful. The world looks different when you are staring at it through bars.

Fool, fool, fool.

What am I doing walking to school with my head in a bird's cage?

Oh no. Here's the school gate. Kids are looking at me. They are pointing. Laughing. Their faces remind me of waves, slapping and slopping at a drowning child.

Strike. Here comes that rotten Philip Noonan. He's grinning. He's poking bits of bread through the bars. 'Pretty Polly,' he says. 'Polly want a biscuit?'

I wish I was an ant so that I could crawl into a crack. Then no one would ever see me.

Teachers are looking out of the staff-room window. I can see Mr Gristle looking. I can see Mr Marsden looking. They are shaking their heads.

I hope Gristle doesn't come. 'Get that thing off your head,' he will shout. 'You idiot. You fool. What do you think you are? A parrot?' Then he will try to rip the cage off my head. He will probably rip the ears off my skull while he is doing it.

Mr Marsden is coming. Thank goodness. He is the best teacher in the school. I don't think he'll yell. Still, you never know with teachers. He hasn't seen a boy come to school with his head in a bird cage before.

'Gary,' he says kindly, 'I think there is something you want to say.'

I shake my head. There is nothing to say. It is too late. I am already a murderer. Nothing can change that.

Mr Marsden takes me inside. We go into the sick bay and sit down on the bed. He looks at me through the bars but he doesn't say anything. He is waiting. He is waiting for me to tell my story.

After a bit I say, 'All right. I'll tell you all about it. But only if you keep it secret.'

Mr Marsden thinks about this for a bit. Then he

smiles and nods his head. I start to tell him my story.

2

On Friday I walk over to see Kim Huntingdale. She lives next door. I am in love with her. She is the most beautiful girl in the world. When she smiles it reminds me of strawberries in the springtime. She makes my stomach go all funny. That's how good she is.

My dog Skip goes with me. Skip is a wimp. She runs around in circles whenever anyone visits. She rolls over on her back and begs for a scratch. She would lick a burglar's hand if one came to rob our house. She will not fight or bark. She runs off if Mum growls. Skip is definitely a wimp.

Mind you, when Mum growls I run off myself. When she is mad it reminds me of a ginger-beer bottle bursting in the fridge.

Anyway, when I get to Kim's house she is feeding Beethoven. Beethoven is her budgie. She keeps it in a cage in the back yard. She loves Beethoven very much. Lucky Beethoven.

Beethoven can't fly because he only has one wing. Kim found him in the forest. This enormous, savage dog had the poor bird in its mouth. Kim grabbed the dog without even thinking of herself and saved Beethoven's life. But he was only left with one wing and he can't fly at all.

Now Kim loves Beethoven more than anything.

I love Skip too. Even though she is a wimp.

Kim looks at Skip. 'You shouldn't bring her over here,' she says. 'Beethoven is scared of dogs.'

Skip rolls over on her back and begs with her four little legs. 'Look at her,' I say. 'She wouldn't hurt Beethoven.' When she rolls over like that Skip reminds me of a dying beetle.

Kim walks into Beethoven's aviary. She lets me in and locks Skip out by putting a brick against the door. Kim picks up Beethoven and the little budgie sits on her finger. It starts to sing. Oh, that bird can sing. It is beautiful. It is magic. A shiver runs up my spine. It reminds me of the feeling you get when fizzy lemonade bubbles go up your nose.

Kim puts the bird down on the ground. It is always on the ground because it can't fly. 'Tie up Skip,' says Kim, 'and I'll let Beethoven out for a walk.'

I do what she says. I would do anything for Kim. I would even roll over on my back and beg like Skip. Just for a smile. But Kim hardly knows I am here. I tie up Skip and Kim lets Beethoven out for a walk. He chirps and sings and walks around the back yard. It reminds me of a little yellow penguin walking around on green snow.

Skip is tied up so she just sits and looks at Beethoven and licks her lips.

3

After a while Kim shuts Beethoven back in the aviary and puts the brick in front of the door. Skip sticks one ear up in the air (the other one won't move) and looks cute. Kim gives her a pat and a cuddle. 'She's a lovely dog,' she says. 'But you have to keep her away from Beethoven.'

'Don't worry,' I say. 'I promise.'

Kim smiles at me again. Then she says something that makes my heart jump. 'Next to Beethoven, you are my best friend.'

It is hard to tell you how I feel when I hear this. My stomach goes all wobbly. It reminds me of a bunch of frogs jumping around inside a bag.

I walk back to our place feeling great. Wonderful. Mum isn't home so I can let Skip inside. Mum doesn't like Skip being in the house. Skip is a smart dog.

She can open the door with her paw if it is left a little bit ajar.

Mum won't let Skip in because she once did a bit of poop under the dresser. It did not smell very nice and I had to clean it up. Skip's poop reminds me a bit of ...

'I think we can miss that bit,' says Mr Marsden who is listening to my story carefully and looking at me through the bars of the bird cage.

'OK,' I say. 'I'll move on to the awful bit.'

4

I do not see Kim for two days because I have to visit Grandma with Mum. We leave Skip at the dog kennels all day Friday and Saturday. When we get back we collect her from the kennels. Poor Skip. She can't even put up one ear. She hates the dog kennels. She cries and whimpers whenever she has to stay there. But she is too scared of the other dogs to bark.

We drive home with Skip on my knee. She looks at me with those big brown eyes. They remind me a bit of two pools of gravy spilt on the tablecloth.

'Skip can sleep inside tonight,' I say to Mum.

'No,' says Mum. 'You tie her up in the shed, the same as always.'

Poor Skip. That night I do not tie her up. I sneak her into my bedroom and let her sleep in bed with me. She is a very clean dog. She is always licking and chewing herself.

Mum, however, has a keen sense of smell. She will know that Skip has been in. Even when you burn incense in your room Mum can still smell dog. I open the window to let in the fresh air. Then I fall asleep and have a lovely dream. All about how Kim and I and Beethoven and Skip get married and all live together on a tropical island. It reminds me a bit of one of those pretend stories that always have a lovely ending. I wish real life was like that.

The next day is Sunday. I sleep in until the sun shines on my face and wakes me up. A soft wind is blowing into the room. I get out of bed and shut the window.

Skip has gone.

5

I look out of the window and see Skip running around with a yellow tennis ball.

I think about how Mum doesn't like getting dog spit on the tennis balls. It leaves green marks on her hands.

Green marks. Our tennis balls are green.

What is that yellow thing in Skip's mouth? I jump out of the window and run down the yard. Skip sees me coming. A chase. She loves a chase. She runs off at top speed. She reminds me a bit of a rabbit bobbing up and down as it runs away from a hunter.

My heart is beating very fast. 'Please,' I say to myself. 'Let it be a ball. Let it be Mum's best glove. Let it be my new transistor radio. But don't let it be ...' It is too awful to even say.

I run after Skip. She loves the fun. She runs under the house. 'Come out,' I yell. 'Come out, you rotten dog.' Skip does not move. 'I'll kill you,' I yell. I am shouting. There are tears in my eyes.

Skip knows that I'm mad. She rolls over on her back and begs. Way under the house where I can't even get her. She drops the yellow thing and nicks off.

Oh, no. I can't bear it. I crawl under the house on my stomach. It is dusty and dirty. There are spiders but I don't even notice them.

I stretch out my hand and I grab the little bundle of feathers. It is Beethoven. Dead. He is smeared with blood and dirt and dog spit. His eyes are white and hard. His little legs are stiff. They remind me of frozen twigs on a bare tree. Beethoven stares at me without seeing. He has sung his last song.

Tears carve tracks down my face. They run into my mouth and I taste salt.

Everything is ruined. My life is over. My dog has killed Beethoven. It is all my fault. If I had tied Skip up this would never have happened. My head swims. When Kim finds out she will cry. She will hate me. She will hate Skip.

Her mum will tell my mum. What will they do to Skip?

6

I crawl out into the back yard. Skip is wagging her tail slowly. She knows something is wrong. I feel funny inside. For a second I feel like kicking Skip hard. I feel like kicking her so hard that she will fly up over the fence.

Then I look into her gravy-pool eyes and I know that she is just a dog. 'Oh, Skip,' I cry. 'Oh, Skip, Skip, Skip. What have you done?' Then I say to myself. 'Gary, Gary, Gary, what have you done?'

I tie Skip up. Then I take Beethoven into my bedroom. He is so small and stiff and shrunken. He reminds me a bit of my own heart.

I think about Kim. She mustn't find out. What if I go and buy another yellow budgie? One that looks the same. She will never know. Kim's car is not there. They are out.

I go down to the garage and get this old golden cage that is covered in dust. When I was a little kid I used to think it was made of real gold. 'No,' Mum told me, 'it is only gilt.'

I wrap up Beethoven in a tissue and put him carefully in my pocket. Then I look in my wallet. Seven dollars. Just enough. I jump on my bike with the golden cage tied to the back. Where do they sell budgies? At the market. It is late. The market will be closing soon.

I ride like I have never ridden before. The wind whips my hair. I puff. I pant. Sweat runs into my eyes. I ride up Wheeler's Hill without getting off my bike. No one has ever ridden up Wheeler's Hill before. My heart is hurting. My legs are aching. I look at my watch. It's five o'clock. The market will be closed.

It is. The trucks are all leaving. The shoppers have

gone. The ground is covered in hot-dog papers and cabbage leaves. The stalls are empty.

I look at the trucks. One or two men are still loading. I drop my bike and run from truck to truck. Car parts – no. Plants – no. Watches – no. Chocolates – no. Candy floss – no. I look in each truck. None has pets.

I am done. I hang my head. Beethoven is dead. Kim will hate me. Kim will hate Skip. What will happen?

I walk back slowly. Men are laughing. Children are calling. Cats are meowing.

Cats are meowing? Pets.

There is a lady with a small van and in the back are cats, dogs, guinea pigs and birds. There is a large cage full of birds.

'Please,' I yell. 'Please. Have you got any budgies?'

'They are up the back of the truck,' she says. 'I can't get them out now. Come back next week.'

'I can't,' I sob. 'I need it now.'

The lady shakes her head and starts up her van. I take Beethoven out of my pocket and unwrap him. The lady looks at the little blood-stained body. She turns off the engine with a sigh and starts to unload the van.

At last we get the cage of birds unloaded. There are canaries and finches. The cage is filled with birds. There are about twenty budgies. There are green ones and blue ones.

And there is one yellow one. It looks just like Beethoven. It is a ringer for Beethoven. I will put this bird in Kim's cage and she will never know the difference.

'Ten dollars,' says the lady. 'Yellow ones are hard to get.'

I empty my wallet. 'I only have seven dollars,' I tell her.

The lady takes my money with a smile and gently hands me the bird. 'I was young once myself,' she says.

I put the bird in my golden cage and pedal like crazy. My trip back reminds me a bit of a sailing boat skidding to shore in a storm. I hope I can get there before Kim arrives home. I have to put the new bird in the cage before she knows Beethoven is dead.

7

Finally I get home. There is no car at Kim's house yet. They are still out. I rush into the back yard and down to the aviary where the wire door is flapping in the wind. The new budgie is sitting on the perch in my golden cage. It flaps its wings.

Wings?

Beethoven only had one wing. Beethoven couldn't fly. Oh no. Kim will know straight away that the new bird is not Beethoven.

My plan has failed. I take out the little bird and stretch out its wings. It has one wing too many. 'Little bird, little bird,' I say. 'You're no good to me like this. What will I do with you?'

There is only one thing to do. I throw the tiny budgie up into the air. 'Goodbye, little bird,' I say. It flies off in a flurry of feathers and disappears for ever.

I go home.

All is lost. Kim will know what Skip has done. Kim will know what I have done. I let Skip run free. I didn't chain her up like Mum told me. It is all my fault. I am a murderer. I am responsible for Beethoven's death.

I will never be able to look at Kim. She will never want to look at me.

Then I get an idea. I'll bury Beethoven and say nothing. Kim will think he has escaped and walked off.

No. That's no good. Kim will still think Skip opened the cage. And she'll ask me to help look for Beethoven. I would have to pretend to hunt for the bird knowing it was dead.

I get another idea. It is better. But terrible. I will sneak back to the cage and put Beethoven inside. I will lock up the cage with the brick. Kim will think that Beethoven has died of old age.

But Beethoven is covered in blood and dirt and dried-up dog spit.

I will have to clean him. I take Beethoven's body to the laundry and wash him gently. I hate myself for doing this. The blood starts to rinse out. But not all of it. I soak him for a while. I try detergent. I try soap. At last he is clean.

He is clean. And dead. And wet.

8

I go and fetch Mum's hair dryer and I dry out Beethoven's feathers until they are all fluffy and new. I gently close his staring eyes. Then, I sneak down to Kim's back yard. I remind myself a bit of a robber skulking around a jewellery shop.

I go inside the aviary door and put Beethoven

down on the sawdust. No one will ever know my terrible secret. I am safe. Skip is safe. Kim will still like us. I close the door, replace the brick and go home.

That night I cannot sleep. I see Kim's sad face. I dream of myself in jail. Nobody likes me. Nobody wants me. I have caused sorrow and pain.

In the morning I look out of my window. I see Kim and her mum and dad. They are gathered around the cage. I can't hear what they are saying. I don't want to know what they are saying. Kim will be crying. Her tears will be falling. If I could see them they would remind me of a salty waterfall.

I see Kim's father put an arm around her shoulder. I wish it could be my arm. I see her mum pick up Beethoven gently in her hand.

I can't look at them any more. Everything is my fault. Poor Skip is just a dog. I should have tied her up. Murderer. I am a murderer. And no one will ever know. My horrible secret will stay with me for ever.

I get the golden cage and rush out to the garage. I cut a hole in the bottom with tin snips. I push my head through the hole. I will wear the golden cage for the rest of my life. It is my punishment. It is what I get for what I did. I will never take it off.

9

Mr Marsden is looking at me sadly. 'You made a mistake,' he says. 'A little mistake that made big things happen. But it wasn't your fault. And even if it was, you can't carry around the burden for ever. Like a rock on your shoulders. Or a cage on your head. You have to face up to it. Tell Kim. And then go on living.'

We are still sitting on the sick-room bed. Looking out of the window. A girl is slowly walking into the school grounds. She is late for school. She reminds me of a lonely ghost.

It is Kim.

Mr Marsden walks out and brings her into the room. Her eyes are red, but still lovely. Her face is sad. It reminds me of a statue of a beautiful princess who has passed away. I cannot look at her. I shrink down in my cage.

'I'm sorry to be late,' she says to Mr Marsden. 'But something happened at home. My budgie Beethoven died on Friday. Dad says he died of old age.'

I hang my head in shame. I can't tell her the truth. I just can't.

Friday?

'Not Friday,' I say. 'Yesterday.'

'No,' says Kim. 'He died on Friday. We buried him in the back yard. But someone dug him up and put him back in the aviary.'

I take the cage off my head and throw it in the bin. After school I walk home with Kim. She holds my hand. It sort of reminds me of, well, flying free, like we are up there in the clouds with Beethoven.

Clear as Mud

I'm undone.

Yes, I know. I'm a fink. A rat. A creep. Nobody likes Eric Mud and it's all my own fault.

But I don't deserve this.

I look in the mirror and see a face that is not a face.

I peel back my gloves and see a hand that is not a hand.

I pull off my socks and see feet that are not feet.

I look down my pants and see ... No, I'm not going to describe that sight.

Oh, merciful heavens. Please, please. I don't deserve this.

Do I?

1

It all began with Osborn. The nerd.

See, he was a brainbox. He always did his homework. He played the piano. He collected insects. The teachers liked him. You know the type.

I spotted him on his first day at school. A new kid. All alone on the end of the bench. Trying not to look worried. Pretending to be interested in what was inside his bright yellow lunch box. Making out that he wasn't worried about sitting by himself.

'Look at it,' I jeered. 'The poor little thing. It's got a lovely lunch box. With Bandaid on it. Has it hurt itself?'

The silly creep looked around the schoolyard. He saw everyone eating out of brown paper bags. No one in this school ever ate out of a lunch box. Especially one with the owner's name written on a Bandaid.

Osborn went red. 'G'day,' he said. 'I'm Nigel Osborn. I'm new here.'

He even held out his hand. What a wimp. I just turned around and walked off. I would have given him a few other things to think about but my mate Simmons had seen something else interesting.

'Look,' yelled Simmons. 'A parka. There's a dag down on the oval wearing a parka.'

We hurried off to stir up the wimp in the parka. And after that we had a bit of fun with a kid covered in pimples.

A few days went by and still Osborn had no friends. Simmons and I made sure of that. One day after school we grabbed him and made him miss his bus. Another time we pinched his glasses and flushed them down the loo.

I never missed a chance to make Osborn's life miserable. He wandered around the schoolyard like a bee in a garden of dead flowers. Completely alone.

Until the day he found the beetle.

2

'A credit to the whole school,' said old Kempy, the school principal. 'Nigel Osborn has brought honour to us, to the town. In fact to the whole nation.'

I couldn't understand what he was raving about. It was only a beetle. And here was the school principal going on as if Osborn had invented ice-cream.

Kempy droned on. 'This is not just a beetle,' he said. 'This is a new beetle. A new species. It has never before been recorded.' He waved the jar at the kids. What a bore.

Everyone except me peered into the bottle.

'It is an ant-eating beetle,' said Kempy. 'It eats live ants.' He looked over at me. 'Eric Mud, pay attention,' he said.

I just yawned loudly and picked my teeth.

At that very moment the beetle grabbed one of the ants that was crawling on the inside wall of the jar. The beetle pushed the ant into its small mouth. It disappeared – legs twitching as it went.

Osborn stood there staring at his shoes, pretending to be modest. What a nerve. He needed to be put back in his box.

But that would have to wait. Old Kempy was still droning on. He stopped and took a deep breath. 'This species will probably be named after Nigel Osborn,' he said. 'Necrophorus Osborn.'

'Necrophorus Nerd Head,' I whispered loudly. A few kids laughed.

Kempy went on with his speech. 'This is the only beetle of its type ever seen. An expert from the museum is coming to fetch it tomorrow. Until then it will be locked in the science room. No one is to enter that room without permission. It would be a tragedy if this beetle were to be lost.'

My mind started to tick over.

A tragedy, eh?

Well, well, well.

3

It was midnight. Dark clouds killed the moon. I wrapped my fist in a towel and smashed it through the window. The sound of broken glass tinkled across the science room floor.

Once inside I flashed a beam of light along the shelves. 'Where are you, beetle? Where are you, little Nerd Head?' I whispered. 'Come to Daddy.'

It was harder than I thought. The science room was crammed with animals in bottles. Snakes, lizards, spiders. There were so many dead creatures that it was hard to find the live one I wanted.

But then I saw it. On the top shelf. A large jar containing a beetle and some ants.

I reached up and then froze. Somewhere in the distance a key turned in a lock. The security guard. Strike. I couldn't get caught. Old Kempy had already warned me. One more bit of trouble and he would kick me out of the school.

I scrambled out of the window. A jagged piece of glass cut my leg. It hurt like crazy but I didn't care. Pain never worries me. I'm not a wimp like Osborn. I ran across the oval and into the dark shadows of the night.

I held the beetle jar above my head. I had done it.

Back home in the safety of my bedroom I examined my prize. The beetle sat still. Watching. Waiting. It was covered in crazy colours – red, green and gold – with black legs. It was about the size of a coat button.

I looked at the ants. They didn't know what was in store for them. Beetle food.

They were queer-looking ants too. I had never seen any like them before. They were sort of clear. You could see right through them. The beetle suddenly grabbed one and ate it. Right in front of my eyes.

It was funny really. This was the only one of these beetles that had ever been found. This could be the last specimen. There might be no more in the world. And in the morning I was going to flush it down the loo. What a joke.

But the next day I changed my mind. There was no hurry. I shoved the jar in the cupboard and went to school.

I played it real cool. I didn't tell anybody what I had done. You never know who you can trust these days.

Old Kempy was not too pleased. In fact he was as mad as a hornet. He gathered the whole school together in the assembly hall.

'Last night,' he said slowly, 'someone broke into the science room and stole our beetle.' His eyes roved over the heads of all the kids. He stopped when he reached me. He stared into my eyes. But I just stared back. He couldn't prove a thing. He was just an old bore.

But his next words weren't boring. Not at all. 'The School Council,' he said, 'is offering a reward of two hundred dollars for information which leads to the arrest of the thief. Or two hundred dollars for another specimen. Nigel Osborn's beetle was found in the National Park. Any beetle hunters should search there.'

Old Kempy looked at Osborn. 'You needn't worry, Nigel,' he said. 'We have photos. The new species will still be named after you.'

Rats. The little wimp was still going to be famous.

I walked home slowly. An idea started to form in my head. What if I kept the beetle for a few weeks? Then I would pretend I found another one in the National Park. No one would know the difference. And I would be famous. They might even name it after me. Necrophorus Mud.

I raced home and grabbed the jar. The ants were gone. Eaten alive.

I tipped the beetle on to the table and picked it up. Its little legs waved helplessly at the ceiling. This was the beetle that was making Osborn famous. I didn't like that beetle. I gave it a squeeze.

And it bit me.

4

I yelled and dropped the beetle on the floor. I was mad. 'You rotten little ...' I said. I lifted up a boot to squash the stupid thing. Then I remembered the two-hundred-dollar reward. I scooped the beetle up and put it back in the jar.

I jumped into bed but couldn't sleep. My finger throbbed where the beetle had bitten me. I had a nightmare. I dreamed that I was the pane of glass in the science room window. And that someone with a towel around their fist punched a hole right through me.

I screamed and sat up in bed. It was morning.

My hand throbbed like crazy. I held it up in front of my face. I couldn't believe what I saw.

A cold wave of fear grabbed my guts. My legs trembled. My heart missed a beat.

I could see right into my finger. From the middle knuckle right down to the tip of my nail was clear. Transparent.

The bones. The tendons. The nerves and blood vessels. I could see them all. It was as if the flesh of my fingertip had changed into clear plastic.

I rubbed my eyes with my other hand. I shook my head. This was a nightmare. 'Let it be a dream,' I moaned. I rushed to the sink and splashed my face with cold water. Then I looked again.

It was still there.

I was a freak with a see-through finger. I felt faint. The room seemed to wobble around me.

No one in the world had a see-through finger. Kids would laugh. Sneer. Joke about me. People are like that. Pick on anyone who is different.

I couldn't tell a soul. Not my old man. Not my old

lady. And especially not Simmons. I couldn't trust him an inch. He would turn on me for sure.

Breakfast was hard to eat with gloves on but I managed it. Then I headed off for school. I stumbled along the road hardly knowing where I was going. I was so upset that I didn't even feel like stirring Jug Ears Jensen. And I hardly noticed the sheila with the pimples. I didn't even have the heart to give a bit of stick to the kid in the parka.

It was just my luck to have Old Kempy for first period. 'I know you're into fashion, Mud,' he said. 'But you might as well face it. You can't use a keyboard with gloves on. Take them off.'

I can tell you my knees started to knock. I couldn't let anyone see my creepy finger. 'Chilblains,' I said. 'I have to wear gloves.'

Old Kempy gave a snort and turned away. I stuck two gloved fingers up behind his back.

5

As soon as the bell rang I bolted into the toilets and shut myself in one of the cubicles. I peeled the glove off my left hand. Perfectly normal. The flesh was pink and firm. Then, with fumbling fingers I ripped off the other glove.

I nearly fainted.

My whole hand was as clear as glass. I could see the tendons pulling. The blood flowing. The bones moving at the joints. Horrible, horrible, horrible. The beetle disease was spreading.

With shaking fingers I ripped at my shirt buttons. I couldn't bear to look. Hideous. Revolting. Disgusting.

I could see my breakfast slowly squirming inside my stomach. My lungs, like two pink bags, filled and emptied as I watched. I stared in horror at my diaphragm pumping up and down. Arteries twisted and coiled. Fluids flowed and sucked. My kidneys slowly swayed like two giant beans.

My guts revealed their terrible secrets. I could see the lot. Bare bones. Flesh. And gushing blood.

I strangled a cry. I felt sick. I rushed to the bowl and heaved. I saw my stomach bloat and shrink. The contents rushed up a transparent tube into my throat and out into the loo.

This was a nightmare.

How much of me was see-through? I inspected every inch of my body. Everything was normal down below. My legs were OK. And my left arm. So far only my stomach, chest and right arm were infected. Blood vessels ran everywhere like fine tree roots.

I wanted to check my back but I couldn't. Simmons and I had smashed the toilet mirrors a couple of weeks ago.

The bell for the next class sounded. I was late but it didn't matter. We had Hancock for English – a new teacher just out of college. He was scared of me. He wouldn't say a thing when I walked in late.

I covered up my lungs, liver, kidneys and bones and headed off for class. So far my secret was safe. Nothing was showing.

All the kids were talking and mucking around. No one was listening to poor old Hancock. He couldn't control the class. One or two kids looked up as I walked in.

Silence spread through the room. Mouths dropped open. Eyeballs bulged. Everyone was staring at me. As if I was a freak.

Jack Mugavin jumped to his feet and let out an enormous scream. Hancock fainted. The class erupted. Running. Rat-scared. Yelling. Scrambling. Scratching. They ripped at the folding doors at the back of the room. Falling over each other. Crushing. Crashing. Anything to get away from me.

What was it? What had they seen? Everything was covered. I checked myself again: hands, feet, ankles, legs, hip, chest, face.

Face?

I rushed to the window and stared at my reflection. A grinning skull stared back. A terrible throbbing spectre. It was tracked with red and purple veins. My jellied nose was lined with wet bristles. A liquid tongue swallowed behind glassy cheeks. My eyeballs glared back at me. They floated inside two black hollows.

That's when I fainted.

6

When I awoke I remembered my dream. Thank goodness it was all over. I grinned with relief and held my hand in front of my face.

I could see straight through it.

I shouted in rage and flopped back on the bed. It wasn't a nightmare. It was real. I ripped away the crisp white sheets. I was dressed in a hospital gown. I pulled it up and examined myself. I was transparent down to the tip of my toes. I was a horrible, see-through, sideshow freak.

I rushed over to the window. A silent crowd had assembled outside. Two police cars were parked by the kerb. Television cameras were pointed my way. The mob stared up at the hospital, trying to catch a glimpse of the unspeakable ghoul inside. Me.

They wanted to dissect me. Discuss me. Display me. I despised them all. Wackers. Wimps. The world was full of them.

The mob would pay hundreds for a photo. Thousands for a story. Maybe millions for an interview. They made me sick.

I knew their type.

I pulled back the curtains and stretched my bare body for all to see. Inside and out. Blood and bone. Gut and gristle. I showed them the lot.

A low moan swept through the crowd. People screamed. Cameras flashed and whirred. Clicking. Clacking. Staring. Shouting.

They leered and laughed. Mocking monsters. Ordinary people.

A doctor hurried into the room carrying a tray. He grabbed me and tried to push me back into bed. But I was too strong for him. I shoved a veined hand into his face and pushed him off. I could feel my fingers inside his mouth. He choked and gurgled as he fell. He scrambled to his feet and fled.

I pulled on my clothes and with shirt flapping swept down the corridor. Nurses, doctors and police grabbed at me weakly. But they had no stomach for it. Like children touching a dead animal they trembled as I passed.

The crowd at the kerb fell back in horror. I raised my arms to the heavens and roared. They turned and ran, dropping cameras and shopping bags. Littering the road with their fear.

I set off down the empty streets. Loping for home. Looking for a lair.

It wasn't far to go. I kicked the front door open and saw my old lady standing there. She tried to scream but nothing came out. She turned and ran for her life. She hadn't even recognized her own son.

I growled to myself. I pushed food into a knapsack. Meat. Bread. Clothes. Boots. A knife.

And the beetle – still in its jar.

I charged out into the backyard and scrambled over the fence.

Then I headed for the mountains.

7

Up I went. Up, up, up into the forest. No one followed. Not at first.

The sun baked the track to powder. The bush waited. Buzzing. Shimmering. Slumbering in the summer heat.

I was heading for the furthest hills. The deepest bush. A place where no one could see my shame. I decided to live in the forest for ever.

No one was going to gawk at me. I hated people who were different. And now I was one of a kind.

When my food ran out I would hunt. There was plenty to eat. Wallabies, possums, snakes. Even lyrebirds.

After five or six hours of trudging through the forest I started to get a strange feeling. Almost as if I was being followed.

Every now and then a stick would break. Once I thought I heard a sort of a howl.

I crawled underneath a fern and waited.

Soon the noises grew louder. I *was* being followed. I grabbed my knife and hunched down ready to spring.

Scatter. Jump. Lollop. Dribble. Would you believe

it was a dog? A rotten half-grown puppy scampered into view.

'Buzz off,' I yelled. 'Scram. Beat it.' The stupid dog jumped around my feet. I kicked out at it but missed. It thought I was playing.

The last thing I wanted was a dog. Yapping and giving me away. I threw a stone at it and missed. The dog yelped off into the bush.

But it didn't give up. It just followed a long way back. In the end I gave up. I could teach it to hunt and kill. It might be useful.

'Come here, Hopeless,' I said.

The stupid thing came and licked my arm. Its tongue flowed along my clear liquid skin. It didn't seem to mind that I was transparent. Dogs don't care if their owners are ugly. Inside or out.

The night fell but I dared not light a fire. I huddled in a blanket inside a hollow tree. Hopeless tried to get in to warm himself but I kicked him out. The mutt probably had fleas.

I found a couple of ants in the wood.

Food.

But not for me. I opened the jar and dropped the ants inside. Then I watched the beetle stuff its dinner into its mouth.

I looked at the beetle with hatred. It had caused all this trouble. I was going to make it pay. 'One day,' I said. 'One day, little beetle, I am going to eat you.'

For three weeks I tramped through the forest. Deeper and deeper. There were no tracks. No signs of human life. Just me and Hopeless. We ate possums and rats and berries. At nights we shivered in caves and under logs.

There were leeches, march flies. Cold. Heat. Dust. Mud. On and on I went. The ugly boy and the stupid dog.

Sometimes I would hear a helicopter. Dogs barking. A faint whistle on the air. But in the end we left them far behind. We were safe. Deep in the deepest forest.

I found a cave. Warm, dry and empty. It looked down on to a clear rushing river. There would be fish for sure.

Hopeless liked the cave too. The stupid mutt ran around sniffing and wagging its tail.

It was the first laugh I'd had for ages. Oh, how I laughed. I cackled till the tears ran down my face. To see that dog wag its tail. Its long clear tail. With the bones showing through the skin. And veins weaving their way in and out.

Hopeless had the see-through disease. What a joke. It was catching.

In the morning most of the dog was see-through. The only bit to stay normal was its head. It had a hairy dog's head but the rest of it was bones, and lungs and kidneys and blood vessels. Just like me. I held up a bit of dead possum. 'Beg,' I said. 'Beg.'

It did too. It sat up and begged. But I didn't give it the possum. There wasn't enough to share around.

8

We stayed in that cave for ten years. The three of us. Me, Hopeless and the beetle. I was like Robinson Crusoe. I set up the cave with home-made furniture. In the end it was quite comfortable.

Every day I fed that beetle. Two ants a day. I kept him alive for ten years – can you believe it? And every day I told the beetle the same thing. 'When I am twenty-four,' I told it. 'I am going to eat you. To celebrate ten years in the bush.'

Not once did I think of going back to civilization. I wasn't going to be a joke. Looked at. Inspected.

And once they found out that the disease was catching no one would come near me anyway. They would lock me up. Put me in quarantine. Examine me like a specimen. I could never go back.

I was fourteen when I went into that forest.

And I was twenty-four when I left it.

See, it happened like this. On my twenty-fourth birthday I decided to have a little party. A special meal just for me. Something I had been looking forward to for many years.

I grabbed the beetle jar and made a speech. 'Beetle,' I said. 'I am an outcast. An ugly see-through monster. I have lived here with you and Hopeless for ten years. In all that time I have not seen a human face. I haven't heard a spoken word. I want to go home but I can't. Now I pass sentence on you. I sentence you to be eaten alive. Come to Daddy, beetle.'

The beetle waved its legs. It almost seemed to know what was going to happen. I tipped it out of the jar and put it inside my mouth. I held up my mirror and watched it roaming about in there. I could see it through my clear, clear cheeks. It sniffed and snuffed. It searched around trying to find a way out. It had a look down the hole at the back but didn't like what it saw. It backed out.

Then it bit me on the tongue.

I screamed and spat the beetle out on to the floor

of the cave. I stamped on it with my boot and squashed it into pulp. Then I rinsed my mouth out with water from the creek. I spat and coughed.

The pain was terrible. My tongue started to swell. I held the mirror up to my face. I stuck out my tongue to get a good look because I couldn't see it properly through my cheeks.

I couldn't see it properly through my cheeks?

I couldn't see it at *all* through my cheeks.

A pinkish blush was spreading over my face. Eyelids. Lips. A nose. My skin was returning to normal. I couldn't see my spine. My skull was covered by normal hair and flesh. My chin sprouted a dark beard.

I just sat there and watched as the normal colour slowly spread over my body. Skin, lovely skin. It moved down my neck. Over my chest. Down my legs.

By the next day I was a regular human being. Not a kidney or lung to be seen. One bite of the beetle had made me see-through. And another had cured me.

I could go home. I looked like everyone else again.

Hopeless came and licked me on the face. I pushed him away with a scream.

The dog was still clear. I could see a bit of bush rat passing through his stomach.

He was still see-through. What if he reinfected me? Turned me back into a creepy horror? He had just licked my face. I might catch the disease back from Hopeless.

I sat down and thought about it. There was no way I was going to go home unless I was completely cured. I decided to stay for another month. Just to be on the safe side.

Every night I slept with Hopeless. I breathed his breath. I even shared his fleas. But nothing happened. I stayed normal. And Hopeless stayed see-through.

You couldn't get the disease twice. It was like measles or mumps. You couldn't catch it again.

Maybe if the beetle bit you again you would get it. But the beetle was dead. There was no way I would ever be a freak again.

I packed up my things and headed for home.

9

This was going to be great. I would be famous. The return of the see-through man. And his dog.

I would be normal. But not Hopeless. He was still

a walking bunch of bones and innards. I could put him on show. Charge hundreds of dollars for a look. People would come from everywhere to see the dog with the see-through stomach. I would be a millionaire in no time. Hopeless was a valuable dog.

It was a tough trip back through the deep undergrowth and rugged mountains.

But finally the day came.

Hopeless and I stood on the edge of a clearing and stared at a building.

It was a little rural school – the type with one teacher and about fifteen kids. It was a perfect place for me to reappear. They would have a phone. They could ring the papers. And the TV.

The man from the mountains could go home in style.

Still, I was worried. I mustn't frighten them. Hopeless was a scary sight. The teacher and kids would never have seen a dog with its guts showing before. I decide to tie Hopeless up. I didn't want anything to happen to him.

But I was too late. Hopeless bounded off across the grass towards the school.

'Come back, you dumb dog,' I yelled. 'Come back or I'll put the boot into you.'

Hopeless didn't take a bit of notice. He charged across the grass and into the school building.

I waited for the screams of horror. Waited for the students to flee out of the building and run down the road. Waited for the yelling and the fainting.

What if the teacher shot Hopeless? I wouldn't have anything to show. A dead dog was no good.

'Don't,' I yelled. 'Don't.' I ran and ran.

Then I stopped outside the window. I heard excited voices.

'Good dog. Good dog,' said a child's voice.

'Here, boy,' said another.

Something was wrong. They weren't scared of him. Surely Hopeless hadn't changed back too. It couldn't happen that quickly.

I charged into the schoolroom.

The teacher and the kids were all patting Hopeless. His guts still swung about in full view. His dinner still swirled in his stomach. The bones in his tail still swished for all to see.

But the kids weren't scared.

Not until they saw me.

A little girl pointed at me and tried to say something. Then they began screaming. Shouting. Clawing at the windows. They were filled with horror.

127

They had never seen anything as horrible as me before.

The teacher could see that the kids were terrified.

'Out the back,' he yelled at the children. 'Quickly.'

The kids charged out of the back door and the teacher followed.

I was alone in the schoolroom.

I looked at the pictures of the see-through people on the walls. I looked at the photos of the see-through people in the text books. In India. In China. And England.

I looked at the photo of our see-through Prime Minister. And America's see-through President.

I stared out of the window at the see-through children running in fear down the road. Followed by a perfectly normal see-through dog.

And I realized then. As I realize now. That I am the only person in the world who has their innards covered by horrible pink skin.

I am still a freak.

And I don't deserve it.

Do I?

The Strap Box Flyer

Hundreds of people were watching Giffen. They thought he was a bit mad. But they couldn't stop looking. He was very interesting.

Giffen went over to his truck and got out a tube of glue. On the tube it said GIFFEN'S GREAT GLUE. IT WILL STICK ANYTHING. Giffen held the glue over his head. 'This is the best glue in the world,' he said. 'It can mend anything that is broken. Who has something that is broken?'

A small boy came out the front. He held up a bow and arrow. 'My bow is broken,' he said. 'And no one can fix it.' Giffen took the bow out of the boy's hand. He put a bit of glue on the broken ends and joined them together. Then he put the arrow in the bow and shot it into the air. The people were surprised. They all clapped and cheered.

'That's nothing,' Giffen told them. 'You haven't seen

anything yet.' He went over to the back of his truck where he had a big crane. It had a rope on the end of it. Giffen grabbed the rope. He put a dab of glue on the end of it. Then he put the rope on to the roof of the car. 'This glue can hold up a car,' he told the crowd. He stepped into his truck and started up the crane. The car was lifted up into the air. The only thing that held the rope on to the car was the glue.

The crowd thought this was great. No one had ever seen glue like this before. 'Now,' said Giffen, 'who wants to buy some of Giffen's Great Glue?'

The crowd rushed forward. Everyone wanted some glue. They couldn't get it quick enough. They thought it was terrific. 'Get it while it lasts,' shouted Giffen. 'Only ten dollars a tube.'

Giffen sold two hundred tubes of glue. He made two thousand dollars in one day. The customers took their glue and went home to try it out.

'You fools,' said Giffen to himself. 'You will soon find out that the glue stops working after four hours.'

2

Miss Tibbs had bought a tube of Giffen's Great Glue. She was a very old lady. She lived all on her own.

Most of her friends were dead. There was no one to help her to fix things up when they got broken. So she was very glad to have the glue.

Miss Tibbs collected china. She had spent all of her life saving pieces of china. She had plates and cups and saucers from all over the world. She also had little china dolls and toy animals. She had so many pieces that she didn't know where to put them all. This is why she wanted the glue. She wanted to put up a new shelf.

As soon as she got home Miss Tibbs went and fetched a piece of wood from the shed in her back garden. Then she put some of Giffen's Great Glue along the edge of the wood and stuck it on to the wall. It worked well. The shelf was very strong.

'This is wonderful glue,' she said. 'It dries straight away.' Miss Tibbs started to put her china pieces on to the shelf. She decided to put her favourite piece out first. It was a small china horse. She had owned it for many years. It had been given to her by her father before he died. Miss Tibbs loved this horse. She put it in the best spot, right in the middle of the shelf.

After she had put all of the other pieces out Miss Tibbs sat down and had a rest. She was very tired. She fell asleep in her armchair in front of the fire.

Four hours later Miss Tibbs was woken up by a loud crash. The glue had stopped working. The shelf had fallen off the wall and all of the china pieces were smashed.

Miss Tibbs went down on to her hands and knees. She started to pick up all of the broken pieces. Then she remembered her horse. Her precious horse. She looked for it among the bits. She couldn't find it. Then she found something that made her cry. A leg and a tail and a tiny head. The horse was smashed to pieces.

Miss Tibbs cried and cried. She got her tube of Giffen's Great Glue and threw it in the fire. Then she decided that she would go and find Giffen. She would tell him that his glue was no good. She would ask him to pay for the broken china.

She hurried back to the place where Giffen had been. But he was gone. There was no sign of him. She knew that he would never come back.

3

Another person who bought a tube of Giffen's Great Glue was Scott Bridges. He had bought it to mend his canoe. It had broken in half.

132

Scott's father had told him the canoe could not be repaired. He said that its back was broken. He told Scott to take it to the tip. But now that Scott had a tube of Giffen's Great Glue he knew that he could fix it.

The canoe was down at the lake. Scott went down there on his own. He didn't tell his father where he was going. He pulled the two pieces of the canoe together, and put Giffen's Great Glue along the join.

'Great,' yelled Scott. 'It's as good as new. This glue is fantastic.' He pushed the canoe into the water and climbed in. It floated well. It didn't leak at all. Scott began to paddle out into the middle of the lake. He was very happy. And excited. He paddled off as fast as he could go.

Scott was not allowed to go out in the canoe without a life jacket. But on this day he had forgotten. All that he could think about was the canoe and Giffen's Great Glue.

It was a sunny day and the time passed quickly. Soon four hours had passed. Scott noticed that some water was starting to leak into the canoe. He decided to start paddling for home. But it was too late. The glue had come unstuck. The canoe broke in two and sank.

The water was icy cold. Scott was frightened. It was a long way to the shore. 'Help,' he screamed at the top of his voice. But no one heard him. He was the only person on the lake.

Scott started to swim to shore. After a little while he began to get tired. His legs hurt and he had a pain in his stomach. His head went under the water. He tried to get to the top. But it was no use. His lungs filled with water and he sank to the bottom of the lake.

That night when Scott did not come home his father called the police. Divers searched the lake. They found Scott's body. And the broken canoe. In the bottom of the canoe was a tube of Giffen's Great Glue.

4

Giffen was driving away in his truck. Very fast. He knew that he only had four hours to get away. Then the people who had bought the glue would start looking for him. He knew that they would be mad. He did not want them to catch him.

He decided to drive to Horsham. That was a long way off. They would not know about Giffen's Great

Glue in Horsham. He could find some more suckers, and make some more money.

Two days later he arrived in Horsham. He took his truck to the centre of town. Then he put up a sign. The sign said:

TWO HUNDRED DOLLARS PRIZE
FOR ANYONE WHO CAN UNSTICK
GIFFEN'S GREAT GLUE

Soon two men arrived. They were both riding tractors. One of the men got down from his tractor. He walked over to Giffen and gave him two pieces of rope. 'Join these up with your glue,' he said. 'Then we will pull it apart.'

Giffen smiled to himself. 'OK,' he said. 'I'll do it.' He put a dob of glue on the ends of the two pieces of rope. Then he joined them together. The glue stuck fast.

The men took the rope that had been joined. They tied one end to each of the tractors. Then they started the tractors up. There was a lot of smoke and noise. A crowd started to gather. Everyone thought that the glue would break. But it didn't. The wheels on the tractors sent up blue smoke. The engines roared. But still the glue held.

Then there was a loud bang. The engine of one of the tractors had stopped. The other tractor started to drag it along the road. Everyone cheered at the top of their voices.

'Now,' said Giffen, 'who will buy my great glue?'

The crowd pushed forward. Everyone wanted some. The people waved their money. They pushed and shoved. Giffen sold three hundred tubes.

At last everyone went home. Except one man. A short, bald man with a friendly smile. 'Excuse me,' he said to Giffen. 'But I wonder if you would like to buy something from me?'

'What are you selling?' said Giffen in gruff voice.

'A Strap Box Flyer. It is a small box that will make people fly.'

5

Giffen didn't believe that there was a box that could make someone fly. There was no such thing. This man was trying to fool him. Still, he was interested. It might be a new sort of trick that he could use himself, to make money from the suckers. He looked at his watch. He had to get out of this town before the glue started to come unstuck. He had four hours left. There was plenty of time to talk to the little man.

'OK,' said Giffen to the little man. 'Show me your Strap Box Flyer.'

'Not here, someone might see us. Come home with me and I will show you how it works.'

Giffen followed the little man home to his house. It was a small cottage. It was very untidy. The grass was long and some of the windows were broken. Inside there was junk everywhere. There were tools, nuts and bolts, machines and bits of wire all over the floor.

'My name is Mr Flint,' said the little man. 'But everyone calls me Flinty.'

'I'm in a hurry, Flinty,' said Giffen. 'So let me see you do some flying.'

'Very well, very well,' replied Flinty. He went over to a shelf and took down a small box. Then he lifted up the carpet and pulled out a short strap. It looked like a watch band made out of silver.

'I keep the strap in one place, and the box in another,' said Flinty. 'That's to stop anyone stealing my invention. I have to screw the box on to the strap. It won't work unless both pieces are screwed together.'

Flinty fiddled around with the box and the strap.

It took a long time. About half an hour. Giffen was getting worried. He did not want to stay much longer. The crowd would be mad when they found out that the glue did not work for long. At last Flinty finished. He had screwed the box on to the strap. He put it on to his arm. It looked just like a wrist watch, only bigger.

'Now,' said Flinty. 'Watch this.' Slowly he rose up off the floor. He went up about ten centimetres.

Giffen could not believe it. His eyes nearly popped out of his head. 'How high can you go?' he asked Flinty.

'As high as I want to.' Flinty floated up to the ceiling. Then he flew around the room, just like a cloud.

Giffen knew that he had to get the Strap Box Flyer. It was worth a fortune. He could make a lot of money if he had it.

6

'Why are you showing this to me?' Giffen asked Flinty.

'Because you are a great inventor,' said Flinty. 'You have invented Giffen's Great Glue. I am an inventor too. I have invented the Strap Box Flyer. We could be partners. You could help me make the Strap Box Flyer. And I could help you to make the glue.'

Giffen did not say anything. He was thinking. He wanted the Strap Box Flyer. But he couldn't stay in Horsham. Once four hours was up his glue would stop working. The things that people had mended would start falling to bits. They would come looking for him. He could even end up in jail.

'Have you got another Strap Box Flyer?' Giffen asked.

'Yes,' said Flinty. 'I have one more. You can try it out if you want to. But first I will have to assemble it. I will have to screw the strap on to the box.'

'That will take half an hour,' said Giffen. 'I will go and get my truck. Then I will be back to try out the Strap Box Flyer myself.' Giffen went off. He had decided to steal the Strap Box Flyer. He wanted to have the truck near by for a quick getaway.

Giffen could not believe his luck. Once he had the Strap Box Flyer he would find out how it worked. Then he would make more of them. He could sell them for thousands of dollars each. He would make a fortune. Everyone would want one.

He ran back to his truck. Then he drove to Flinty's house as fast as he could. The Strap Box Flyer was ready. There would just be time for a quick tryout and then he would have to leave town.

Flinty put the Strap Box Flyer on to Giffen's arm. 'Now,' he said. 'All you have to do is to think of where you would like to fly to.'

Giffen thought that he would like to fly over to his truck. It worked. He went gently flying through the air and landed on the roof of his truck. Flinty floated over and joined him. 'Great,' said Giffen. 'Really great. How high can we go with these things?'

'As high as you like,' said Flinty. 'As high as you like.'

7

Giffen forgot about everything except the Strap Box Flyer. He forgot about the time. He forgot about Giffen's Great Glue and he forgot about getting out of town quickly.

'Let's go up to the clouds,' he said to Flinty. And so they flew together. High into the sky. When they looked down the people looked like tiny ants. It was wonderful to fly so high.

Time passed quickly. Hours went by. It started to get dark. Giffen decided that he would wait until it was night. Then he would be able to get away from Flinty. He would just fly off and lose Flinty in the dark. Then he would drive off in his truck and never come back. He could take the Strap Box Flyer to bits and find out how it worked. Then he could make a lot more of them. And sell them. Then he would be rich.

Flinty flew over to Giffen. 'We are very high,' he said. 'We can't go much higher than this. There will be no air to breathe.'

Giffen looked down. They were so high that he could not see the ground. They were above the clouds.

'I have only made two Strap Box Flyers so far,' said Flinty, 'and yours is the best of the two.'

'Why is that?' asked Giffen.

'Because I joined it together with Giffen's Great Glue.'

Giffen was just in time to see his Strap Box Flyer break into bits. Then he started to fall.

He screamed all the way down.

The Copy

I was rapt. It was the best day of my life. I had asked
Fiona to go with me and she said yes. I couldn't
believe it. I mean it wasn't as if I was a great catch.
I was skinny, weak, and not too smart at school.
Mostly I got Cs and Ds for marks. And I couldn't
play sport at all. I hated football, always went out
on the first ball at cricket and didn't know which
end to hold a tennis racquet. And Fiona had still said
she'd be my girlfriend.

Every boy in year eleven at Hamilton High would
be jealous. Especially Mat Hodson. It was no secret
that he fancied Fiona too. I grinned to myself. I
wished I could see his face when he found out the
news. He thought that he was so great and in a way
he was. He was the exact opposite to me. He was
smart (always got As for everything), captain of the
footy team, the best batsman in the cricket team and

he was tough. Real tough. He could flatten me with one punch if he wanted to. I just hoped he took it with good grace about Fiona and me. I didn't want him for an enemy.

I headed off to Crankshaft Alley to see my old friend Dr Woolley. I always went to see him when something good happened. Or something bad. I felt sort of safe and happy inside his untidy old workshop and it was fun seeing what crazy thing he was inventing. Everything he had come up with so far had been a flop. His last invention was warm clothes pegs to stop people getting cold fingers when they hung out the clothes. They worked all right but no one would buy them because they cost two hundred dollars each. All of his inventions had turned out like that. They worked and they were clever but they were too expensive for people to buy.

I walked on down past all the other little shop-front factories until I reached Dr Woolley's grubby door. I gave the secret knock (three slow, three fast) and his gnomish face appeared at the window. I say gnomish because he looked just like a gnome: he was short with a hooked nose and he had a white beard and a bald head surrounded with a ring of white hair. If you gave him a fishing rod and a red cap and sat him in the front yard you would think he was a little garden statue.

He opened the door. 'Come in Rodney,' he said.

'Tim,' I corrected. He always called me the wrong name. He had a terrible memory.

'Where's that screwdriver?' he said. 'It's always getting lost.'

'In your hand,' I told him.

'Thanks, Peter, thanks.'

'Tim,' I sighed. I don't know why I bothered. He was never going to call me by my right name. It wasn't that he didn't know who I was. He did. I was his only friend. Everyone else thought he was a dangerous crackpot because he chased them away from his front door with a broken mop. I was the only person allowed into his workshop.

'Are you still working on the Cloner?' I asked.

His face turned grim and he furtively looked over at the window. 'Sh ... Not so loud. Someone might hear. I've almost perfected it. I'm nearly there. And this time it is going to pay off.' He led me across the room to a machine that looked something like a telephone box with a whole lot of wires hanging out of it. Down one side were a number of dials and switches. There were two red buttons. One was labelled COPY and the other REVERSE.

Dr Woolley placed a pine cone on the floor of the Cloner. Then he pressed the button that said COPY. There was a whirring sound and a puff of smoke and then, amazingly, the outline of another pine cone, exactly the same as the first, appeared. It lasted for about ten seconds and then the machine started to rock and shake and the whirring slowly died. The image of the second pine cone faded away.

'Fantastic,' I yelled.

'Blast,' said Dr Woolley. 'It's unstable. It won't hold the copy. But I'm nearly there. I think I know how to fix it.'

'What will you use it for?' I asked. 'What's the good of copying pine cones? There are plenty of pine cones already. We don't need more of those.'

He started to get excited. 'Listen, Robert.'

'Tim,' I said.

'Tim, then. It doesn't only work with pine cones. It will work with anything.' He looked up at the window as he said it. Then he dropped his voice. 'What if I made a copy of a bar of gold, eh? What then? And then another copy and another and another. We would be rich. Rich.'

145

I started to get excited too. I liked the way he said 'we'.

Doctor Woolley started nodding his little head up and down. 'All I need is time,' he said. 'Time to get the adjustment right. Then we will show them whether I'm a crank or not.'

We had a cup of tea together and then I headed off home. That was two good things that had happened in one day. First, Fiona saying she would go with me and second, the Cloner was nearly working. I whistled all the way home.

I didn't see Dr Woolley for some time after that. I had a lot on my mind. I had to walk home with Fiona and every night I went to her place to study with her. Not that we got much study done. On weekends we went hiking or hung around listening to records. It was the best time of my life. There was only one blot on the horizon. Mat Hodson. One of his mates had told me he was out to get me. He left a message saying he was going to flatten me for taking his girl.

His girl! Fiona couldn't stand him. She told me she thought he was a show-off and a bully. But that wasn't going to help me. If he wanted to flatten me he would get me in the end. Fortunately he had caught the mumps and had to stay at home for three weeks. Someone had told me it was very painful.

I decided to go round to see Dr Woolley about a month later. I wondered if he had perfected his Cloner. When I reached the door I gave the secret knock but there was no answer. 'That's strange,' I said to myself. 'He never goes out for anything.'

I looked through the window and although the curtains were drawn I could see the light was on inside. I knocked again on the door but still no answer. Then I started to worry. What if he had had a heart attack or something? He could be lying unconscious on the floor. I ran around to the back, got the key from the hiding spot in an old kettle and let myself into the workshop. The place was in a mess. Tables and chairs were turned over and crockery was lying smashed on the floor. It looked as if there had been a fight in the workshop. There was no sign of Dr Woolley.

I started to clean the place up, turning the chairs up the right way and putting the broken things into the bin. That's when I found the letter. It was in an envelope marked with four names. It said, 'John', 'Peter', 'Robert', and 'Tim'. The first three names were crossed out. Dr Woolley had finally remembered my name was Tim after four tries. Inside the letter said:

TIM
IF YOU FIND THIS LETTER SOMETHING
TERRIBLE HAS HAPPENED. YOU MUST
DESTROY THE CLONER AT ONCE.
WOOLLEY

My eye caught something else on the floor. I went over and picked it up. It was another letter exactly the same as the first. Exactly the same. It even had the three wrong names crossed out. Dr Woolley really was the most absent-minded person.

I looked at the Cloner with a feeling of dread. What had happened? Why did he want me to destroy it? And where was Dr Woolley? The Cloner was switched on. I could tell that because the red light next to REVERSE was shining. I walked over to it and switched it over to COPY. I don't know what made me do it. I guess I just wanted to know if the Cloner worked. I should have left it alone but I didn't. I took a Biro out of my top pocket and threw it inside the Cloner.

Immediately an image of another Biro formed. There were two of them where before there had only been one. I turned the Cloner off and picked up both pens. As far as I could tell they were identical. I couldn't tell which was the real one. They were both real.

I sat down on a chair feeling a bit dizzy. This was the most fantastic machine that had ever been invented. It could make me rich. Dr Woolley had said that it could even copy gold bars. All sorts of wonderful ideas came into my mind. I decided that nothing would make me destroy the Cloner.

I went over and switched the machine on to REVERSE. Then I threw both of the pens into the Cloner. I was shocked by what happened. Both of them disappeared. They were gone. For good. I turned it back to COPY but nothing happened. I tried REVERSE again but still nothing. It was then that I noticed a huge blowfly buzzing around the room. It flew crazily around my head and then headed straight into the Cloner. It vanished without a trace.

The Cloner was dangerous when it was switched on to REVERSE. It could make things vanish for good. I wondered if Dr Woolley had fallen into the machine. Or had he been pushed? There were certainly signs of a struggle.

I thought about going to the Police. But what could they do? They couldn't help Dr Woolley if he had fallen into the Cloner. And they would take it away and I would never see it again. I didn't want that to happen. I had plans for that machine. It was mine now. I was the rightful owner. After all, Dr Woolley had said that 'we' would be rich. Unfortunately now it was just going to be me who was rich.

I went back to Fiona's house and spent the evening doing homework with her. I didn't tell her about the Cloner. I was going to give her the first copies I made from it. At ten o'clock I walked home through the darkened streets, keeping an eye out for Mat Hodson. I had heard he was over his mumps and was looking for me.

The next morning I borrowed Mum's gold cameo brooch without telling her. I decided not to go to school but instead I went to Dr Woolley's workshop. Once inside I turned the Cloner on to COPY and threw in the brooch. Immediately another one appeared. I turned the Cloner off and took out both brooches. One was a mirror image of the other. They both had the same gold setting and the same ivory face. But on one brooch the face looked to the left and on the other it looked to the right. Apart from that they were identical.

I whistled to myself. The copy was so good I couldn't remember which way Mum's brooch had faced. Still it didn't matter. I would put one of them back where I had got it and give the other to Fiona.

Next I decided to experiment with something that was alive. I went outside and hunted around in the long grass. After a while I found a small green frog with a black patch on its left side. I took it in and threw it straight into the Cloner. In a flash there were two frogs. They jumped out on to the workshop floor. I picked them up and looked at them. They were both alive and perfectly happy. They were both green but one had a black patch on the left and the other had it on the right. One was a mirror image of the other.

This Cloner was wonderful. I spent all day there making copies of everything I could think of. By four o'clock there was two of almost everything in the workshop. I decided it was time to go and give Fiona her cameo. She was going to be very happy to get it.

I never made it to Fiona's house. An unpleasant

surprise was waiting outside for me. It was Mat Hodson.

'I've been waiting for you, you little fink,' he said. 'I heard you were hiding in here.' He had a pair of footy boots hanging around his neck. He was on his way to practise. He gave a nasty leer. 'I thought I told you to stay away from my girl.'

'She's not your girl,' I said hotly. 'She can't stand you. She's my ...' I never finished the sentence. He hit me with a tremendous punch in the guts and I went down like an exploding balloon. The pain was terrible and I couldn't breathe. I fought for air but nothing happened. I was winded. And all I could do was lay there on the footpath wriggling like a dying worm.

'You get one of those every day,' he said. 'Until you break it off with Fiona.' Then he laughed and went off to footy practice.

After a while my breath started to come back in great sobs and spasms. I staggered back into the workshop and sat down. I was mad. I was out of my mind. I had to think of some way to stop him. I couldn't go through this every day and I couldn't give up Fiona. I needed help. And badly. But I couldn't think of anyone. I didn't have a friend who would help me fight Hodson except Fiona and I couldn't ask her.

My mind was in a whirl and my stomach ached like crazy. I wasn't thinking straight. That's why I did the stupidest thing of my life. I decided to get inside the Cloner and turn it on. There would be two of me. Two Tims. I could get The Copy to help me fight Hodson. He would help me. After all, he would be the same as me. He would want to pay Hodson back as much as I did. The more I thought about it, the smarter it seemed.

I would make an exact copy of myself and together we could go off and flatten Hodson. I wondered what my first words to the new arrival should be. In the end I decided to say, 'Hello there, welcome to earth.' I know it sounds corny but at the time it was all I could think of.

I turned the Cloner to COPY and jumped in before I lost my nerve. In a twinkling there was another 'me' standing there. It was just like looking into a mirror. He had the same jeans, the same jumper and the same brown eyes. We both stood staring at each other for about thirty seconds without saying a thing. Then, both at the same time we said, 'Hello, there, welcome to earth.'

153

That gave me a heck of a shock. How did he know what I was going to say? I couldn't figure it out. It wasn't until much later I realized he knew all about me. He had an exact copy of my brain. He knew everything I had ever done. He knew what I had been thinking before I stepped into the Cloner. That's why he was able to say the same sentence. He knew everything about me. He even knew how many times I had kissed Fiona. The Copy wasn't just a copy. He was me.

We both stood there again for about thirty seconds with our brains ticking over. We were both trying to make sense of the situation. I drew a breath to say something but he beat me to it. 'Well,' he said. 'What are we waiting for? Let's go get Hodson.'

The Copy and I jogged along the street towards the football ground without speaking. I wondered what he was thinking. He didn't know what I was thinking. We shared the same past but not the same future or present. From now on everything that happened would be experienced differently by both of us. I didn't have the faintest idea what was going on in his head. But I knew what was going on in mine. I was wondering how I was going to get rid of him when this was all over.

'Fiona will like that brooch,' said The Copy. I was shocked to think he knew about it. He was smiling to himself. I went red. He was probably thinking Fiona was going to give him a nice big kiss when she saw that brooch. It was me she was going to kiss, not The Copy.

At last we reached the football ground. Hodson was just coming out of the changing rooms. 'Well look,' he said. 'It's little Tim and his twin brother. Brought him to help you, have you?' he said to The Copy. 'Well, I can handle both of you.' He screwed up his hand into a tight fist. Suddenly he looked very big. In fact he looked big enough to wipe the floor with both of us.

I felt like running for it. So did The Copy. I could see he was just about to turn around and run off, leaving me on my own. We both turned and fled. Hodson chased after us for a bit and finally gave it away. 'See you tomorrow, boys,' he yelled. I could hear the other footballers laughing at us. It was humiliating. I knew the others would tell Fiona about what a coward I was.

I turned to The Copy. 'A fat lot of use you turned out to be,' I said.

'What are you talking about?' he replied. 'You're

the one who turned and ran off first. You knew I couldn't handle him on my own.'

I realized The Copy was a liar. I decided to go home for tea. He walked along beside me. 'Where do you think you're going?' I asked.

'Home for tea.'

'We can't both turn up for tea. What's Mum going to say when she sees two of us? The shock will kill her,' I told him.

We both kept on walking towards home. The Copy knew the way. He knew everything I knew. Except what I was thinking. He only knew about what had happened before he came out of the Cloner. He didn't know what was going on in my mind after that. I stopped. He seemed determined to come home with me. 'Look,' I said. 'Be reasonable. Think of Mum and Dad. We can't both sit down for tea. You go somewhere else.'

'No,' he said. 'You go somewhere else.'

Finally we came to the front gate. 'All right,' I said to The Copy. 'You go and hide in the bedroom. I'll go down to tea and afterwards I'll sneak you up some food.'

The Copy didn't like it. 'I've got a better idea,' he told me. 'You hide in the bedroom and I'll bring you up something.'

I could see he was only thinking of himself. This thing was turning into a nightmare. 'All right,' I said in the end. 'You go down to tea and I'll hide in the bedroom.' So that is what we did. I sneaked up and hid in my room while The Copy had tea with my parents. It was roast pork. My favourite. I could smell it from my room and it smelt delicious.

The sound of laughter and chattering floated up the stairs. No one knew The Copy wasn't me. They couldn't tell the difference. A bit later he came up the stairs. He poked his head around the corner and threw me a couple of dry biscuits. 'This is all I could find. I'll try and bring you up something later.'

Dry biscuits. I had to eat dry biscuits while The Copy finished off my tea. And I just remembered Mum had been cooking apple pie before we left. This was too much. Something had to be done.

Just then the doorbell rang. 'I'll get it,' shouted The Copy before I had a chance to open my mouth. He ran down the stairs and answered the door. I was trapped. I couldn't go down or Mum and Dad would see there were two of us.

I could hear a girl's voice. It was Fiona. A bit later the door closed and all was silent. The Copy had

157

gone outside with her. I raced over to the window and looked out. It was dark but I could just see them under the wattle tree. The street light illuminated the scene. What I saw made my blood boil. The Copy was kissing Fiona. He was kissing my girlfriend. She thought he was me. She couldn't tell the difference and she was letting the creep kiss her. And what is worse she seemed to be enjoying it. It was a very long kiss.

I sat down and thought about the situation. The Copy had to be sent back to where he came from. This whole thing had turned out to be a terrible mistake. I had to get The Copy back to the workshop and get rid of him.

After about two hours The Copy came up to the bedroom looking very pleased with himself. I bit my tongue and didn't say anything about him kissing Fiona. 'Look,' I said. 'We can't both stay here. Why don't we go back to the workshop and have a good talk. Then we can figure out what to do.'

He thought about it for a bit and then he said, 'OK, you're right. We had better work something out.'

I snuck out of the window and met him outside. We walked all the way to the workshop in silence.

I could tell he didn't like me any more than I liked him.

I took the key out of the kettle and let us in. I noticed the Cloner was still switched on to copy. I went over and turned it on to REVERSE without saying anything. It would all be over quickly. He wouldn't know what hit him. I would just push him straight into the Cloner and everything would be back to normal. He would be gone and there would be just me. It wouldn't be murder. I mean he had only been alive for a few hours and he wasn't really a person. He was just a copy.

'Look,' I said, pointing to the floor of the Cloner. 'Look at this.' I got ready to push him straight in when he came over.

The Copy came over for a look. Suddenly he grabbed me and started to push me towards the machine. The Copy was trying to kill me. He was trying to push me into the Cloner and have Fiona for himself. We fell to the floor in a struggling heap. It was a terrible fight. We both had exactly the same strength and the same experience. As we fought I realized what had happened to Dr Woolley. He had made a copy of himself and they had both tried to push each other in. That's why there were two letters.

Probably they had both fallen in and killed each other.

The Copy and I fought for about ten minutes. Neither of us could get the upper hand and we were both growing tired. We rolled over near the bench and I noticed an iron bar on the floor. But The Copy had noticed it too. We both tried to reach it at the same time. But I won. I grabbed it and wrenched my arm free. With a great whack I crashed it down over The Copy's head. He fell to the floor in a heap.

I dragged his lifeless body over to the Cloner and shoved him inside. He vanished without a trace. It was just as if he had never existed. A feeling of great relief spread over me but I was shaking at the narrow escape I had experienced. I turned and ran home without even locking up the workshop.

By the time I got home I felt a lot better. I walked into the lounge where Mum and Dad were sitting watching TV. Dad looked up at me. 'Ah there you are, Tim. Would you fill out this application for the school camp? You put in the details and I'll sign the bottom.'

I took the form and started to fill it in. I was looking forward to the school camp. We were going skiing. After a while I looked up. Mum and Dad were both staring at me in a funny way.

'What's up?' I asked.

'You're writing with your left hand,' said Dad.

'So?'

'You've been a right hander all your life.'

'And your hair is parted on the wrong side,' said Mum. 'And that little mole that used to be on your right cheek has moved to the left side.'

My head started to swim. I ran over to the mirror on the wall. The face that stared back at me was not Tim's. It was the face of The Copy.

Thought Full

'I am never eating meat again,' I yelled at Dad.

He just smiled at me as if I was crazy.

You might think I'm crazy too. I mean most people who live on farms eat meat. So I'll tell you what. You be me for a while and see how you feel about it at the end.

1

It all starts because of the new steer. We have this cow called Slipped-in-the-Mud and it gives birth down in the bottom paddock. To the sweetest little calf you have ever seen.

The calf has a cute white patch on its face. It sucks away at its mother's udder and gets white froth all around its mouth.

And it likes you. It nuzzles up for a pat. Oh, it is

so wonderful. It moos in a real soft way. It looks at you with those big brown eyes. Straight away you decide to call it Moonbeam.

You have never loved anything like you love this little calf.

'Dad,' you say. 'Can Moonbeam be mine? To keep for ever? Just mine? Please.'

Dad shakes his head sadly. 'Sorry, Bomber,' he says. 'We can't afford to have it eating grass and not earning its way. Once it's weaned we have to sell it.'

'There's plenty of grass around here,' you yell.

'No there's not,' says Dad. 'We need every blade for the heifers who are going to give us milk. Steers do not grow up into cows. They become bulls. And they eat plenty.'

Tears fill your eyes. You just can't stand it. 'I won't let him go,' you shout. But deep in your heart you know that you are only a kid. You have no power. There is nothing you can do to stop them selling Moonbeam. You run off to your room and bang the door. You are so angry that you don't come out for at least five minutes.

The next day is really the start of all the weird things that happen. You wake up in the morning to find a terrible smell in the room. In the bed in fact. You look at your hands and give a scream. Your hands are all covered in sloppy, green slime.

It stinks something terrible. How did it get there? Is someone playing a trick? What is going on here? Where did this horrible stuff come from? It looks like the goo that bubbles in the bog down by the front gate.

You think about it for a while and decide not to tell Mum and Dad about it. But it is too late. Mum is already in your bedroom and she is not rapt in what she sees.

'I told you to have a shower last night,' says Mum angrily. 'Look, your sheets are all dirty. They're covered in green slime.'

'I did have a shower,' you say. 'Honest.'

You can tell that Mum doesn't believe you. You find it hard to believe yourself. How could your hands have got so dirty when you were asleep in bed all night?

You don't worry too much about it though because you have Moonbeam to think about. You take a walk down to his paddock for a visit. He is the best friend that you have ever had. When he licks your hand it is like being rubbed with soft, wet sandpaper. You put your arms around his neck. 'I will never let them sell you,' you say.

Suddenly you notice Dad standing behind you. 'Don't keep going on about it, Bomber,' he says. 'Every animal on a farm has to earn its keep. Moonbeam has to go. Times are bad and we need every penny we can get.'

Moonbeam sucks your fingers. He is only a calf. It is not his fault that he was born a male. Your heart is breaking because Moonbeam is going to be sold.

You worry about it all day and on into the evening. It is so bad that you find it hard to get to sleep that night. You toss and turn and try to hatch up plans to save your calf. In the end you nod off into dreamland.

2

At seven o'clock you are awakened by a smell. It is not the whiff of eggs and bacon sizzling in the kitchen. It is not the smell of toast. It is not the scent of a warm, summer morning. It is the stink of slimy mud. You look under the blankets. You are soaked in it. Your pyjama trousers and top. Your feet and hands.

A terrible, squelching, green ooze. The sheets are soaked.

Your brain freezes. Someone must have sneaked into the room and dumped sloppy mud on you. But who? Mum and Dad would never do such a thing.

You grab the sheets and try to sneak down to the laundry with them before Mum sees the mess.

But you are too late.

Mum catches you. At first she doesn't say anything. She just stares at you with one of those looks that says, 'How could you, Bomber?'

She calls a family conference.

This is the very worst thing. Family conferences are for times when the three of you have to work through a problem. 'Communicating,' says Mum.

But what it really means is that you get a big lecture.

'I slave away in that laundry,' says Mum. 'And Dad does the ironing. And what do you do, Bomber? You wander around outside in bare feet and make the sheets filthy. Now is that fair? I ask you.'

You start to give your side of the story. 'But I haven't been outside. I don't even remember ...'

Dad doesn't wait for you to finish. 'It's that silly calf,' he says. 'The boy is going down the paddock talking to the calf in the middle of the night. It's not good enough, Bomber. As soon as that calf is weaned I'm taking it to the market.'

'But ...' you start to say.

'No buts,' says Dad. 'That calf has to go.'

Nothing will change his mind. Usually Dad is reasonable. He is a great father. But nothing will make him believe that you have not been down with Moonbeam in the middle of the night.

This is ruining your life. What is going on? How are you getting dirty in your own bed? Something has to be done. And quick.

That night you go to bed as usual. Well, not quite as usual. You get your alarm clock and tie it around your neck. Then you set it for one o'clock in the morning. If someone is dumping mud in your bed you are going to be awake to catch them.

Finally you fall asleep.

3

No sooner have your eyes closed than, 'Ding, ding, ding, ding.' What a racket. The alarm makes a terrible noise. Straight away you wake up and find out that it is one o'clock.

But where are you? Everything is dark around you. Overhead there are pinpoints of light. What are they doing there on the ceiling? You look again. There is no ceiling. The lights are stars. You are outside in the cold, still night.

The wind is fresh on your cheek. The water is wet on your arms and legs.

Water?

Is this some terrible dream? No, it is not. Worst luck. Your heart sinks. You know where you are.

You are on your hands and knees scratching in the bog down by the front gate. You are covered in green gunk.

Oh no. What is going on here? Why are you outside? You must be sleepwalking. Sleepdigging. This is terrible. Horrible.

You quickly start off towards the house. But you feel uneasy. You keep looking back at the bog. It seems to be calling you. Your feet want to take you back to the disgusting, bubbling slime. It is almost as if a magnet is pulling you back. You have this terrible urge to turn around and dig in the bog.

But you are strong. You don't go. The feeling gets weaker as you move away from the bog. But it is still there all the same. Like a silent voice in your mind calling.

Just as you reach the front door you hear noise from the barn. A moo. Moonbeam.

'What the heck,' you say. 'I might as well go and check on him while I'm here.'

You sneak into the barn and see Moonbeam curled up in the hay. Oh, he is beautiful. You start to stroke his soft, brown coat. You don't think of anything but wonderful Moonbeam. You do not realize that someone else is there too.

A hand falls on your shoulder and you just about jump out of your skin.

'Bomber. What are you doing here?'

It is Dad.

Your mind starts to race. What can you tell him? This looks bad. 'I was sleepdigging,' you say 'In the bog. That's where all the slime is coming from.'

Dad does not believe you. That is clear. 'Bomber,' he says. 'Don't give me that. You are sneaking out to see Moonbeam. You have used up your last chance. I am definitely taking him to the market on Saturday. This has to stop. Now get back to bed.'

'But, but ...'

It is no good. You can see by his eyes that, as usual, no buts are allowed.

You have a shower and get back into bed. You lie there thinking. Dad is going to take Moonbeam to the market. But Moonbeam is not weaned yet. How will he get milk without Slipped-in-the-Mud?

4

Dad doesn't want Moonbeam because he is no good for milk. Why would anyone else buy him? There is a nasty thought in the back of your mind but you can't work out what it is.

Because.

The bog is calling.

Your hands pull back the sheets. Your legs touch the floor. Your feet take you across the room. You don't want to go but you can't stop yourself. The bog. The bog. The bog.

Out into the night. Past the milking shed. Along the track to the front gate.

You find yourself staring into the slime. Frogs are croaking. Green bubbles are floating on the surface. The smell is revolting.

In your mind you scream to yourself, 'No, no, no.'

You try to hold back. You try not to go. Your head feels as if it is filling up with water and is going to burst. The pressure is unbearable.

Suddenly you leap forward. You don't want to go but you can't stop yourself. You hit the water with an enormous splash. You fall on to your hands and knees and start digging with your fingers. You are crazy. Green water sprays everywhere. You are soaked. What are you looking for? You don't know. You don't care. Dig, dig, dig, dig. That is all you can do.

Your fingers touch something smooth. You grab it. And then it happens.

All the madness falls away. Now you are full of peace. You are happy. A wonderful feeling washes all over you. You have found it.

A bottle.

A small bottle covered in mud.

You give it a wash and tip out the bog water. The night is dark and you can't see it properly. Is this what it is all about? The sleepwalking. The digging. Just for a bottle?

Rain begins to fall so you head back to the farmhouse.

Where Dad is waiting on the front step.

He doesn't say anything. He just stands there glaring at you. He is angry. Boy, is he mad. He looks at your soaked pyjamas. He thinks you have been down to see Moonbeam again.

You hold up the bottle and try to explain. 'Er, sleepdigging. The bog was calling. Found this ...'

Dad points upstairs. He only says one word.

'Bed.'

5

You scamper inside as quick as you can go. You have another shower and while you are there you give the bottle a good wash.

It is just made of glass but it sure looks odd. On the bottom is strange writing. On the sides are moons and stars and bunches of grapes. The neck is swollen and shaped like the head of a witch.

You have seen a bottle like this before. It is a baby's bottle. Without the teat. But it is not a normal bottle. No way.

You fill it up with water.

Now it just needs a cap. A little teat. You sneak down to the junk cupboard and find the bottle that Mum used to feed you with when you were a baby.

You take off the teat and put it on the witch bottle. Now it is complete. The teat is just like a hat on the witch's head.

You give a smile and put it under your pillow. In ten seconds you are fast asleep.

The next morning Mum and Dad do not say anything about the sleepdigging. They just stare at you without talking. They shake their heads and look at each other sadly. They are giving you the silent treatment. They are trying to make you feel guilty. And it is working.

You decide that you had better not mention the bottle. Not under the circumstances. You jump in the car and wait for Dad to drive you to school.

He is taking his time so you decide to have a little drink from the witch's hat. Just one sip. It can't do any harm. It is only water after all.

You suck away on the bottle just like a baby. The water tastes a bit strange. Bitter and sweet at the same time. Suddenly things start to happen. The countryside seems different. Colours are brighter. The wind is fresher. Bird songs are sweeter.

But not everything is an improvement. The smell from the milking shed is worse. And the bog seems to bubble and seethe with more gunk than before.

The world is bigger and bolder. A little shiver runs up your spine.

Dad steps into the car and starts off. He is thinking about Moonbeam.

He is thinking about Moonbeam?

How do you know? Because you can read his mind. That's how.

You shake your head. You whack your skull with the palm of your hand. Are you going crazy or what? When you drink out of the bottle you can read people's minds.

You know every thought that Dad is thinking. He is planning to sell Moonbeam at next Saturday's sale.

'Please don't sell Moonbeam on Saturday, Dad,' you say.

Dad gives you a funny look. 'How did …?' But he does not finish the sentence. 'We have to, Bomber,' he says.

'Who will buy him?' you say. 'What if it's not someone nice? What if they don't love him like I do?'

Dad doesn't say anything. But a word comes into his mind. The word is 'veal'.

'What's veal?' you ask.

Dad gives you another strange look. 'It's meat,' he answers.

'What sort of meat?' you say.

Dad doesn't say anything. He doesn't have to. You already know what is in his mind. Veal is the meat of young calves. Your heart stops inside you. Now you know why he doesn't have to wait for Moonbeam to be weaned.

'No,' you scream. 'No, no, no. You can't send Moonbeam off to be slaughtered.'

'Look, Bomber,' says Dad. 'You had bacon for breakfast. Where do you think that came from?'

'That's different,' you yell. 'Moonbeam is almost human. He has a name. Moonbeam loves me.'

Dad sighs. 'Most vealers end up on the table,' he says.

You feel a lump in your throat. Someone eating Moonbeam. You can't stand to think about it. 'I am never eating meat again,' you yell.

Dad doesn't say any more. But he keeps thinking. And you know what he is thinking because you had a drink from the bottle and can read his thoughts. He is feeling sorry for you. But he thinks that life on a farm is tough. And that you will have to get used to it. He thinks that he will take Moonbeam off to a neighbour's farm after you are asleep tonight. Then he will go to the sale yards from there.

But it won't work. Because you know what the plan is. You will keep sucking from the bottle and you will know what Dad is planning to do. You will know what he is going to do before he does it. You will know his every thought. You will always be able to save Moonbeam by outsmarting Dad.

6

Dad drops you off at the school gate. Now that you have a plan you start to settle down.

So. You can read people's minds. This is going to be fun.

The first person you see is The Bot. His real name is James Blessing but everyone calls him The Bot because he borrows from people and doesn't ever pay them back.

Straight away you know what he is thinking. It is amazing. You know what is going on inside his head. He has two all-day suckers in his pocket and he is going to sneak off behind the bike shed and eat one where no one can see.

'Hey, Bot,' you yell. 'How about one of those all-day suckers?'

He goes red in the face. A few kids gather round. 'I ain't got none,' he lies.

'In your pocket,' you say. 'In your left pocket.'

A couple of kids grab him and turn out his pocket. Sure enough – two all-day suckers. The Bot goes red and hands you one.

This is great. Knowing what people think is fun. You start to lick the all-day sucker. You are very pleased with yourself.

Until you realize what The Bot is thinking. He is thinking about how his Dad is out of work. How the family doesn't have much money. How he never gets sweets like the other kids. How he was going to give the all-day sucker to his little sister.

Suddenly you feel mean. And to make it worse you know that he is thinking about how he hates being called The Bot.

He doesn't like people thinking he is stingy. He is embarrassed because his parents can't buy him things.

You wish you hadn't taken the all-day sucker. 'Hey, James. You can have it back,' you say.

But he just shakes his head sadly. It is too late

because you have licked the all-day sucker and its colours are running.

The bell goes and everyone troops into school.

Mr Richards is in a bad mood. You know this because you can read his mind. He is thinking about how his car had a flat tyre this morning. He is thinking that anyone who did not do their homework is going to be in big trouble.

Your heart almost stops. You have not done your homework. What with all the trouble about Moonbeam you clean forgot about it.

On the other side of the room Alan Chan is checking over his answers. The homework is one of those rotten things where you read a sheet and then tick the right answers at the end.

You look at your blank sheet. You can tell what Alan Chan is thinking. He is a brain. He will get them all right. You start to tick the answers with his thoughts. Number one, A. Number two, C. And so on. It is a bit hard to get all of his thoughts because everyone else is thinking things too.

Sue Ellen is thinking about how she loves Peter Elliot.

Peter Elliot is thinking about the pimple on his nose. He is hoping that no one notices it.

Janice Roberts is also thinking about the pimple. She feels sorry for Peter Elliot because she loves him too.

Rhonda Jefferson is thinking about her dying grandma. She is very sad. She is trying to blink back the tears. You start to feel sad and have to blink back the tears too.

All of these thoughts are like static on the radio. They make it hard to tune in to Alan Chan. But in the end you check off all the answers that run through Alan Chan's brain.

7

Mr Richards corrects the homework. He looks at the class.

'Stand up, Bomber,' he says.

Your heart sinks but you stand up anyway.

'And Alan Chan,' says Mr Richards.

Alan stands up too.

'These two boys,' says Mr Richards, 'got everything right. Well done, boys.'

You give a big grin. Usually you have to stand up for getting nothing right. Four other kids have to stay in after school for not doing their homework.

You wonder how Alan Chan is feeling. It doesn't take long to find out. After all, you are a mind-reader.

Alan is feeling tired. He is thinking about how he is not smart like everyone says. He is remembering how he stayed up all night doing his homework. He wishes that he really was a brain like everyone says.

You start to feel a bit mean.

Reading minds may not be as good as you think. And there are other problems. Everyone is thinking. Everyone.

The thoughts of all the class start to crowd in on you. Kids are thinking about sore feet, peanut-butter sandwiches, the flies on the ceiling, the swimming pool, what they had for breakfast, putting out the garbage bin and how they need to go to the loo.

Most of the thoughts are boring. Some are sad. Some are things that you know you should not know. You block your ears but that is no good. The thoughts still come pouring in. It is almost painful. You want peace from all the thoughts. It is so much of a babble that it starts to drive you crazy.

Everyone's daydreams come pouring in. Most of them are about nothing important. Shoe polish. Clouds. Drains. Lollies. Fleas. The beach. Stomach-ache. Hardly anyone is thinking about the lessons.

Mr Richards is wishing the bell would go so that he can have a cup of coffee.

Thoughts, thoughts, thoughts. Noisy, nice, nasty, private and painful. You can't stop the thoughts. The room is quiet but your brain is bursting with it all. You clap your hands over your ears but still the thoughts buzz inside your brain like a billion blowflies.

You can't stand it.

'Shut up,' you yell at the top of your voice.

Everyone looks up.

'Stop thinking,' you yell.

The room was already quiet. But now it is deadly silent.

The kids all think you have gone crackers.

Mr Richards gives you a lecture. 'Thinking,' he says, 'is what school is all about. You could try it more often, Bomber.'

You are sent out into the playground to pick up papers until you learn some manners.

At least there are no thoughts out there in the yard. Except your own.

You think about all the private things you have learned. It is like spying. It is dangerous. You find out things that you don't want to know. It is like peeping through keyholes. It is like cheating in an exam.

There is only one thing to do. The witch bottle is not to be trusted. It could cause fights. Or wars.

The bottle must never be given to another person. You are certainly not going to suck it again and neither is anyone else. Maybe you should smash it up.

You hold up the bottle in your right hand. You swear a little promise to yourself. 'I will never drink from this bottle again,' you say. 'Or I hope to die.'

You are called back into class. The thoughts grow fainter and fainter. By home time you can't tell what anyone is thinking. You are glad that it has worn off. There is no way that you are going to break your oath.

Dad picks you up at the school gate.

You wonder what he is planning. It is probably about how he is going to sell your calf.

When you get home you go down and visit Moonbeam. Oh, he is lovely. Slipped-in-the-Mud gives him a lick.

You try to think of a way to save Moonbeam. Should you suck the bottle again and try to work out what Dad is up to?

No, never. And anyway, you have sworn a sacred oath.

But Dad will catch him. And sell him. To the knackery. You think of veal. It is too horrible. If you suck the bottle you will know what Dad is up to. You can save your calf. But you can't do it. Tears come to your eyes.

You go down to the paddock to say your last goodbyes. After tea Dad tries to catch Moonbeam.

He has him cornered in the barn. He approaches with a rope. He holds out the loop.

But Moonbeam slips past him and runs into the darkening paddock. You smile to yourself. In fact you smile all evening. And the following day. Dad just can't catch Moonbeam no matter how hard he tries.

Finally, after trying all week, Dad comes rushing into the kitchen and throws his rope on to the floor. He is hot and sweaty. He is flustered. He has been chasing Moonbeam for three hours.

'We might as well keep the silly calf,' says Dad. 'I'll never catch it. It gets away every time. It's almost as if it can read your mind.'

No is Yes

The question is: did the girl kill her own father? Some say yes and some say no.

Linda doesn't look like a murderess.

She walks calmly up the steps of the high school stage. She shakes the mayor's hand and receives her award. Top of the school. She moves over to the microphone to make her speech of acceptance. She is seventeen, beautiful and in love. Her words are delicate, musical crystals falling upon receptive ears. The crowd rewards her clarity with loud applause but it passes her by. She is seeking a face among the visitors in the front row. She finds what she is looking for and her eyes meet those of a young man. They both smile.

He knows the answer.

*

'It's finally finished,' said Dr Scrape. 'After fourteen years of research it is finished.' He tapped the thick manuscript on the table. 'And you, Ralph, will be the first to see the results.'

They were sitting in the lounge watching the sun lower itself once more into the grave of another day.

Ralph didn't seem quite sure what to say. He was unsure of himself. In the end he came out with. 'Fourteen years is a lot of work. What's it all about?'

Dr Scrape stroked his pointed little beard and leaned across the coffee table. 'Tell me,' he said, 'as a layman, how did you learn to speak? How did you learn the words and grammar of the English language?'

'Give us a go,' said Ralph good naturedly. 'I haven't had an education like you. I haven't been to university. I didn't even finish high school. I don't know about stuff like that. You're the one with all the brains. You tell me. How did I learn to speak?'

When Ralph said, 'You're the one with all the brains,' Dr Scrape smiled to himself and nodded wisely. 'Have a guess then,' he insisted.

'Me mother. Me mother taught me to talk.'

'No.'

'Me father then.'

'No.'

'Then who?' asked Ralph with a tinge of annoyance.

'Nobody taught you,' exclaimed Dr Scrape. 'Nobody teaches children to talk. They just learn it by listening. If the baby is in China it will learn Chinese because that's what it hears. If you get a new-born Chinese baby and bring it here it will learn to speak English not Chinese. Just by listening to those around it.'

'What's that got to do with your re ...?' began Ralph. But he stopped. Dr Scrape's daughter entered the room with a tray. She was a delicate, pale girl of about fourteen. Her face reminded Ralph of a porcelain doll. He was struck by both her beauty and her shyness.

'This is my daughter, Linda,' said Dr Scrape with a flourish.

'G'day,' said Ralph awkwardly.

'And this is Mr Pickering.'

She made no reply at first but simply stood there staring at him as if he were a creature from another planet. He felt like some exotic animal in the zoo which was of total fascination to someone on the other side of the bars.

Dr Scrape frowned and the girl suddenly remembered her manners.

186

'How do you do?' she said awkwardly. 'Would you like some coffee?'

'Thanks a lot,' said Ralph.

'White or black?'

'Black, thanks.'

Linda raised an eyebrow at her father. 'The usual for me,' he said with a smirk. Ralph Pickering watched as Linda poured two cups of tea and put milk into both of them. She looked up, smiled and handed him one of the cups.

'Thanks a lot,' he said again.

'Salt?' she asked, proferring a bowl filled with white crystals.

Ralph looked at the bowl with a red face. He felt uncomfortable in this elegant house. He didn't know the right way to act. He didn't have the right manners. He didn't know why he had been asked in for a cup of coffee. He was just the apprentice plumber here to fix the drains. He looked down at his grubby overalls and mud-encrusted shoes.

'Er, eh?' said Ralph.

'Salt?' she asked again holding out the bowl.

Ralph shook his head with embarrassment. Did they really have salt in their tea? He sipped from the delicate china cup. He liked coffee, black and with

187

sugar, in a nice big mug. Somehow he had ended up with white tea, no sugar and a fragile cup which rattled in his big hands.

He had the feeling, though, that Linda had not meant to embarrass him. If there was any malevolence it came from Dr Scrape who was grinning hugely at Ralph's discomfort.

Ralph Pickering scratched his head with his broken fingernails.

The young girl looked at her watch. 'Will you be staying for breakfast?' she asked Ralph kindly. 'We are having roast pork. It's nearly washed.'

'N-n-no thanks,' he stumbled. 'My mum is expecting me home for tea. I couldn't stay the night.' He noticed a puzzled expression on her face and she shook her head as if not quite understanding him. The oddest feeling came over him that she thought he was a bit mad.

Ralph moved as if to stand up.

'Don't go yet,' said Dr Scrape. 'I haven't finished telling you about my research. Although you have already seen some of it.' He nodded towards his daughter who had gone into the kitchen and could be heard preparing the pork for the evening meal. 'Now where were we?' he went on. 'Ah yes. About learning to speak. So you see, my dear boy, we learn to speak just from hearing those around us talking.' He was waving his hands around as if delivering a lecture to a large audience. His eyes lit up with excitement. 'But ask yourself this. What if a child was born and never heard anyone speak except on the television? Never ever saw a real human being, only the television? Would the television do just as well as live people? Could they learn to talk then?'

He paused, not really expecting Ralph to say anything. Then he answered his own question. 'No one knows,' he exclaimed thrusting a finger into the air. 'It's never been done.'

'It would be cruel,' said Ralph, suddenly forgetting his shyness. 'You couldn't bring up a child who had never heard anyone speak. It'd be a dirty trick. That's why it's never been done.'

'Right,' yelled Dr Scrape. His little beard was waggling away as he spoke. 'So I did the next best thing. I never let her hear anybody speak except me.' He nodded towards the kitchen.

'You mean ...' began Ralph.

'Yes, yes. Linda. My daughter. She has never heard anyone in the world speak except me. You are the first person apart from me she has ever spoken to.'

189

'You mean she has never been to school?'

'No.'

'Or kindergarten?'

'No.'

'Or shopping or to the beach?'

'No, she's never been out of this house.'

'But why?' asked Ralph angrily. 'What for?'

'It's an experiment, boy. She has learned a lot of words incorrectly. Just by listening to me use the wrong words. All without a single lesson. I call "up" "down" and "down" "up". I call "sugar" "salt". "Yes" is "no" and "no is yes". It's been going on ever since she was a baby. I have taught her thousands of words incorrectly. She thinks that room in there is called the laundry,' he yelled pointing to the kitchen. 'I have let her watch television every day and all day but it makes no difference. She can't get it right.'

He picked up a spoon and chuckled. 'She calls this a carpet. And this,' he said holding up a fork, 'she calls a chicken. Even when she sees a chicken on television she doesn't wake up. She doesn't change. She doesn't notice it. It proves my hypothesis: point that is,' he added for the benefit of Ralph whom he considered to be an idiot. 'So you see, I have made a big breakthrough. I have proved that humans can't learn to speak properly from listening to television. Real people are needed.'

'You know something,' said Ralph slowly. 'If this is true, if you have really taught the poor kid all the wrong words ...'

Dr Scrape interrupted. 'Of course it's true. Of course it's true.' He took out a worn exercise book and flipped over the pages. 'Here they are. Over two thousand words – all learned incorrectly. Usually the opposites. Whenever I talk with Linda I use these words. She doesn't know the difference. Dog is cat, tree is lamp post, ant is elephant and just for fun girl is boy – she calls herself a boy although of course she knows she is the opposite sex to you. She would call you a girl.' He gave a low, devilish laugh.

Ralph's anger had completely swamped his shyness and his feeling of awkwardness caused by the splendour of the mansion. 'You are a dirty mongrel,' he said quietly. 'The poor thing has never met another person but you – and what a low specimen you are. And you've mixed her all up. How is she going to get on in the real world?'

'You mean in on the real world, not on in the real world,' he smirked. Then he began to laugh. He thought it was a great joke. 'You'll have to get used to it,' he said. 'When you talk to her you'll have to get used to everything being back to front.'

'What's it got to do with me?'

'Why, I want you to try her out. Talk to her. See how she goes. Before I give my paper and show her to the world I want to make sure that it lasts. That she won't break down and start speaking correctly with strangers. I want you to be the first test. I want a common working man … boy,' he corrected. 'One who can't pull any linguistic tricks.'

'Leave me out of it,' said Ralph forcefully. 'I don't want any part of it. It's cruel and, and,' he searched around for a word. 'Rotten,' he spat out.

Scrape grabbed his arm and spun him round. He was dribbling with false sincerity. 'But if you really care, if you really care about her you will try to help. Go on,' he said pushing Ralph towards the kitchen. 'Tell her what a despicable creature I am. Tell her the difference between salt and sugar. Set her straight. That's the least you can do. Or don't you care at all?' He narrowed his eyes.

Ralph pushed him off and strode towards the kitchen. Then he stopped and addressed Scrape who had been following enthusiastically. 'You don't come then. I talk to her alone. Just me and her.'

The little man stroked his beard thoughtfully. 'A good idea,' he said finally. 'A good idea. They will want an independent trial. They might think I am signalling her. A good thought, boy. But I will be close by. I will be in here, in the library. She calls it the toilet,' he added gleefully. Then he burst into a sleazy cackle.

Ralph gave him a look of disgust and then turned and pushed into the kitchen.

Linda turned round from where she was washing the dishes and took several steps backwards. Her face was even paler than before. Ralph understood now that she was frightened of him. Finally, however, she summoned up her courage and stepped forward, holding out her hand. 'Goodbye,' she said in a shaking voice.

'Goodbye?' queried Ralph. 'You want me to go?'

'Yes,' she said, shaking her head as she spoke.

Ralph took her outstretched hand and shook it. It was not a handshake that said goodbye. It was warm and welcoming.

'Is this really the first time you have been alone with another person other than him?' asked Ralph, nodding towards the library.

'Don't call him a person,' she said with a hint of

annoyance. 'We don't let persons in the laundry. Only animals are allowed here. The cats have kennels in the river.'

'You've got everything back to front,' said Ralph incredulously. 'All your words are mixed up.'

'Front to back,' she corrected, staring at him with a puzzled face. 'And you are the one with everything mixed down. You talk strangely. Are you drunk? I have heard that women behave strangely when they are drunk.'

Ralph's head began to spin. He couldn't take it all in. He didn't trust himself to speak. He remembered Dr Scrape's words, 'Dog is cat, tree is lamp post, ant is elephant, and just for fun, boy is girl.' Linda was looking at him as if he was mad. He walked over to the sink and picked up a fork. 'What's this?' he said, waving it around excitedly.

'A chicken of course,' she answered. Ralph could see by her look that she thought he was the one with the crazy speech.

'And what lays eggs and goes cluck, cluck?' He flapped his arms like wings as he said it.

The girl smiled with amusement. 'A fork. Haven't you ever seen a fork scratching for bananas?'

Ralph hung his head in his hands. 'Oh no,' he

groaned. 'The swine has really mucked you up. You have got everything back to front – front to back. They don't dig for bananas. They dig for worms.' He stared at her with pity-filled eyes. She was completely confused. She was also the most beautiful girl he had ever seen. He bit his knuckles and thought over the situation carefully. 'Man' was 'woman'. 'Boy' was 'girl'. 'Ceiling' was 'floor'. But some words were right. 'Him' and 'her' were both correct. Suddenly he turned and ran from the room. He returned a second later holding Dr Scrape's exercise book. He flicked wildly through the pages, groaning and shaking his head as he read.

The girl looked frightened. She held her head up like a deer sniffing the wind. 'That glass must not be read,' she whispered, looking nervously towards the library. 'None of the glasses in the toilet can be read either.'

He ignored her fear. 'Now,' he said to himself. 'Let's try again.' He held the exercise book open in one hand for reference. Then he said slowly, 'Have you ever spoken to a girl like me before?'

'Yes,' said Linda shaking her head.

Ralph sighed and then tried again. He held up the fork. 'Is this a chicken?'

'No,' she said nodding her head. Ralph could see

that she was regarding him with a mixture of fear, amusement and, yes, he would say, affection. Despite her bewilderment over what she considered to be his strange speech, she liked him.

Suddenly the enormity of the crime that had been worked on this girl overwhelmed Ralph. He was filled with anger and pity. And disgust with Dr Scrape. Linda had never been to school. Never spoken to another person. Never been to the movies or a disco. For fourteen years she had spoken only to that monster Scrape. She had been a prisoner in this house. She had never been touched by another person ... never been kissed.

Their eyes met for an instant but the exchange was put to flight by the sound of coughing coming from the library.

'Quick,' said Ralph. 'There isn't much time. I want you to nod for "yes" and shake your head for "no" – drat, I mean the other way around.' He consulted the exercise book. 'I mean nod your head for "no" and shake your head for "yes".' He looked again at the book. The words were alphabetically listed. He couldn't be sure that she understood. What if the word for head was foot? Or the word for shake was dance, or something worse?

Linda paused and then nodded.

He tried again. 'Have you ever spoken to another animal except him?' he said jerking a contemptuous thumb in the direction of the library.

She shook her head sadly. It was true then. Scrape's story was true.

'Would you like to?' he asked slowly after finding that 'like' was not listed in the book.

She paused, looked a little fearful, and then keeping her eyes on his, nodded her head slowly.

'Tonight,' he whispered, and then, checking the book, 'No, today. At midnight, no sorry, midday. I will meet you. By that lamp post.' He pointed out of the window and across the rolling lawns of the mansion. 'By that lamp post. Do you understand?'

Linda followed his gaze. There was a lamp post at the far end of the driveway which could just be seen through the leaves of a large gum tree in the middle of the lawn. He took her hand. It was warm and soft and sent a current of happiness up his arm. He asked her again in a whisper. 'Do you understand?'

She nodded and for the first time he noticed a sparkle in her eyes.

'I didn't ask you to maul my son,' a voice hissed from behind them. Ralph jumped as a grip of steel took hold of his arm. Dr Scrape was incredibly strong. He dragged Ralph out of the kitchen and into the lounge. 'You stay in the laundry,' he snarled at Linda as the kitchen door swung closed in her face.

'Well, my boy,' he said with a twisted grin. 'How did it go? Could you make head or tail of what she said? Or should I say tail or head?' He licked his greasy moustache with satisfaction at his little joke.

Ralph tried to disguise the contempt he felt. 'What would happen if she mixed with people in the real world?' he asked. 'If she was to leave here and go to school? Would she learn to talk normally?'

Dr Scrape paused and looked carefully at Ralph as if reading his mind. 'Yes,' he said. 'Of course she would. She would model on the others. She would soon speak just like you I suspect. But that's not going to happen, is it?'

Ralph could contain himself no longer. 'You devil,' he yelled. 'You've mucked her up all right. She thinks I am the one who can't talk properly. She thinks I'm a bit crazy. But don't think I'm going to help you. I'll do everything I can to stop you. You're nothing but a vicious, crazy little monster.' He stood up and stormed out of the house.

Dr Scrape gave a wicked smile of satisfaction as Ralph disappeared down the long driveway.

It was thirty minutes past midnight and a few stars appeared occasionally when the drifting clouds allowed them to penetrate.

It was a different Ralph who stood waiting beneath the lamp post. Gone were the overalls, work boots and the smudged face. He wore his best jeans and his hair shone in the light of the street light. He had taken a lot of time over his appearance.

He looked anxiously at his watch and then up at the dark house. There was no sign of Linda. She was thirty minutes late. His heart sank as slowly and surely as the sun had done that evening. She wasn't coming. She had dismissed him as a funny-speaking crank. Or that evil man had guessed their plan and locked her in a room.

It began to drizzle and soon trickles of water ran down his neck. One o'clock and still no sign of her. He sighed and decided to go. There was nothing more he could do. She wasn't going to show up. The words started to keep time with his feet as he crunched homewards along the gravel road. 'Show up, show up.' Linda would have said 'show down' not 'show up'.

A bell rang in the back of his mind. A tiny, insistent bell of alarm. Once again he heard Dr Scrape speaking. 'Dog is cat, tree is lamp post, ant is …' Of course.

'Tree is lamp post. And therefore … lamp post is tree.' He almost shouted the words out. She called a lamp post a tree. Linda might have been waiting beneath the gum tree in the middle of the gardens while he was waiting under the lamp post by the gate. He hardly dared hope. He ran blindly in the dark night. Several times he fell over. Once he put a hole in the knee of his jeans but he didn't give it a thought.

He knew that she would have gone. Like him she would have given up waiting and have returned to the dark house.

At last he stumbled up to the tree, finding it by its silhouette against the black sky. 'Linda,' he whispered urgently, using her name for the first time. It tasted sweet on his lips.

There was no answer.

Then, at the foot of the house, in the distance, he saw a flicker of yellow light. It looked like a candle. He saw Linda, faintly, holding the small flame. Before he could call out she opened the front door and disappeared inside.

'Damn and blast,' he said aloud. He smashed his clenched fist into the trunk of the tree in disappointment. A lump of bitter anguish welled up in his throat. He threw himself heavily down on the damp ground to wait. Perhaps she would try again. Anyway, he resolved to stay there until morning.

Inside the dark house Linda made her way back to her bedroom upstairs. Her eyes were wet with tears of rejection. The strange girl had not come. She crept silently, terrified of awaking her tormentor. Holding the forbidden candle in her left hand she tiptoed up the stairs. She held her breath as she reached the landing lest her guardian should feel its gentle breeze even from behind closed doors.

'Betrayed, betrayed,' shrieked a figure from the darkness. The candle was struck from her hand and spiralled over the handrail to the floor below. It spluttered dimly in the depths.

The dark form of Dr Scrape began slapping Linda's frail cheeks. Over and over he slapped, accompanying every blow with the same shrill word. 'Betrayed, betrayed, betrayed.'

In fear, in shock, in desperation, the girl pushed at the swaying shadow. Losing his footing, Scrape tumbled backwards, over and over, down the wooden staircase. He came to a halt halfway down and lay still.

Linda collapsed on to the top step, sobbing into her hands, not noticing the smoke swirling up from below. Then, awakened to her peril by the crackling flames that raced up the stairs, she filled her lungs with smoke-filled air, screamed and fainted dead away.

The old mansion was soon burning like a house of straws. Flames leapt from the windows and leaked from the tiles. Smoke danced before the moonless sky.

The roar of falling timber awakened Ralph from a fitful doze at the base of the tree. He ran, blindly, wildly, unthinkingly through the blazing front door and through the swirling smoke, made out Linda's crumpled form at the top of the staircase. He ran to her, jumping three steps at a time, ignoring the scorching flames and not feeling the licking pain on his legs. Staggering, grunting, breathing smoke he struggled with her limp body past the unconscious form of Dr Scrape. He paused, and saw in that second that Scrape was still breathing and that his eyes were wide and staring. He seemed unable to move. Ralph charged past him, forward, through the burning door and along the winding driveway. Only the sight of an ambulance and fire truck allowed him to let go and fall with his precious load, unconscious on the wet grass.

'Smoke inhalation,' yelled the ambulance driver. 'Get oxygen and put them both in the back.'

Linda's eyes flickered open and she stared in awe from the stretcher at the uniformed figure. Only the third person she had seen in her life. A mask was lowered over her face, but not before she had time to notice that the unconscious Ralph was breathing quietly on the stretcher next to her.

'I want to speak to her,' yelled the fire chief striding over from the flashing truck.

'No way, they are both going to hospital,' shouted the ambulance driver in answer.

The fire chief ignored the reply and tore the mask from Linda's gasping mouth. He bent close to her. 'I can't send men in there,' he yelled, pointing at the blazing house. 'Not unless there is someone inside. Is there anyone inside?'

'Mother,' whispered the girl.

The fireman looked around. 'She said mother.'

'She hasn't got a mother,' said a short bald man who had come over from the house next door. 'Her mother died when the girl was born. She only has a father. Dr Scrape.'

The fireman leaned closer. His words were urgent. 'Is your father in there, girl? Is anyone in there? The roof is about to collapse. Is anyone inside the house?'

Linda tried to make sense of his strange speech. Then a look of enlightenment swept across her face. She understood the question – that was clear. But many have wondered if she understood her own answer.

As the ambulance driver shut the door she just had time to say one word.

'No.'

Wunderpants

My Dad is not a bad sort of bloke. There are plenty who are much worse. But he does rave on a bit, like if you get muddy when you are catching frogs, or rip your jeans when you are building a tree hut. Stuff like that.

Mostly we understand each other and I can handle him. What he doesn't know doesn't hurt him. If he knew that I kept Snot, my pet rabbit, under the bed, he wouldn't like it; so I don't tell him. That way he is happy, I am happy and Snot is happy.

There are only problems when he finds out what has been going on. Like the time that I wanted to see *Mad Max II*. The old man said it was a bad movie – too much blood and guts.

'It's too violent,' he said.

'But, Dad, that's not fair. All the other kids are going. I'll be the only one in the school who hasn't seen it.' I went on and on like this. I kept nagging. In the end he gave in – he wasn't a bad old boy. He usually let me have what I wanted after a while. It was easy to get around him.

The trouble started the next morning. He was cleaning his teeth in the bathroom, making noises, humming and gurgling – you know the sort of thing. Suddenly he stopped. Everything went quiet. Then he came into the kitchen. There was toothpaste all around his mouth; he looked like a mad tiger. He was frothing at the mouth.

'What's this?' he said. He was waving his toothbrush about. 'What's this on my toothbrush?' Little grey hairs were sticking out of it. 'How did these hairs get on my toothbrush? Did you have my toothbrush, David?'

He was starting to get mad. I didn't know whether to own up or not. Parents always tell you that if you own up they will let you off. They say that they won't do anything if you are honest – no punishment.

I decided to give it a try. 'Yes,' I said. 'I used it yesterday.'

He still had toothpaste on his mouth. He couldn't talk properly. 'What are these little grey hairs?' he asked.

'I used it to brush my pet mouse,' I answered.

'Your what?' he screamed.

'My mouse.'

He started jumping up and down and screaming. He ran around in circles holding his throat, then he ran into the bathroom and started washing his mouth out. There was a lot of splashing and gurgling. He was acting like a madman.

I didn't know what all the fuss was about. All that yelling just over a few mouse hairs.

After a while he came back into the kitchen. He kept opening and shutting his mouth as if he could taste something bad. He had a mean look in his eye – real mean.

'What are you thinking of?' he yelled at the top of his voice. 'Are you crazy or something? Are you trying to kill me? Don't you know that mice carry germs? They are filthy things. I'll probably die of some terrible disease.'

He went on and on like this for ages. Then he said, 'And don't think that you are going to see *Mad Max II*. You can sit at home and think how stupid it is to brush a mouse with someone else's toothbrush.'

2

I went back to my room to get dressed. Dad just didn't understand about that mouse. It was a special mouse, a very special mouse indeed. It was going to make me a lot of money: fifty dollars, in fact. Every year there was a mouse race in Smith's barn. The prize was fifty dollars. And my mouse, Swift Sam, had a good chance of winning. But I had to look after him. That's why I brushed him with a toothbrush.

I knew that Swift Sam could beat every other mouse except one. There was one mouse I wasn't sure about. It was called Mugger and it was owned by Scrag Murphy, the toughest kid in the town. I had never seen his mouse, but I knew it was fast. Scrag Murphy fed it on a special diet.

That is what I was thinking about as I dressed. I went over to the cupboard to get a pair of underpants. There were none there. 'Hey, Mum,' I yelled out. 'I am out of underpants.'

Mum came into the room holding something terrible. Horrible. It was a pair of home-made underpants. 'I made these for you, David,' she said. 'I bought the material at the Op Shop. There was just the right amount of material for one pair of underpants.'

'I'm not wearing those,' I told her. 'No way. Never.'

'What's wrong with them?' said Mum. She sounded hurt.

'They're pink,' I said. 'And they've got little pictures of fairies on them. I couldn't wear them. Everyone would laugh. I would be the laughing stock of the school.'

Underpants with fairies on them and pink. I nearly freaked out. I thought about what Scrag Murphy would say if he ever heard about them. I went red just thinking about it.

Just then Dad poked his head into the room. He still had that mean look in his eye. He was remembering the toothbrush. 'What's going on now?' he asked in a black voice.

'Nothing,' I said. 'I was just thanking Mum for making me these nice underpants.' I pulled on the fairy pants and quickly covered them up with my jeans. At least no one else would know I had them on. That was one thing to be thankful for.

The underpants felt strange. They made me tingle all over. And my head felt light. There was something not quite right about those underpants – and I am not talking about the fairies.

3

I had breakfast and went out to the front gate. Pete was waiting for me. He is my best mate; we always walk to school together. 'Have you got your running shoes?' he asked.

'Oh no,' I groaned. 'I forgot. It's the cross-country race today.' I went back and got my running shoes. I came back out walking very slowly. I was thinking about the race. I would have to go to the changing rooms and get changed in front of Scrag Murphy and all the other boys. They would all laugh their heads off when they saw my fairy underpants.

We walked through the park on the way to school. There was a big lake in the middle. 'Let's chuck some stones,' said Pete. 'See who can throw the furthest.' I didn't even answer. I was feeling weak in the stomach. 'What's the matter with you?' he asked. 'You look like death warmed up.'

I looked around. There was no one else in the park. 'Look at this,' I said. I undid my fly and showed Pete the underpants. His eyes bugged out like organ stops; then he started to laugh. He fell over on the grass and laughed his silly head off. Tears rolled down his cheeks. He really thought it was funny. Some friend.

After a while Pete stopped laughing. 'You poor thing,' he said. 'What are you going to do? Scrag Murphy and the others will never let you forget it.'

We started throwing stones into the lake. I didn't try very hard. My heart wasn't in it. 'Hey,' said Pete. 'That was a good shot. It went right over to the other side.' He was right. The stone had reached the other side of the lake. No one had ever done that before; it was too far.

I picked up another stone. This time I threw as hard as I could. The stone went right over the lake and disappeared over some trees. 'Wow,' yelled Pete. 'That's the best shot I've ever seen. No one can throw that far.' He looked at me in a funny way.

My skin was all tingling. 'I feel strong,' I said. 'I feel as if I can do anything.' I went over to a park bench. It was a large concrete one. I lifted it up with one hand. I held it high over my head. I couldn't believe it.

Pete just stood there with his mouth hanging open.

He couldn't believe it either. I felt great. I jumped for joy. I sailed high into the air. I went up three metres. 'What a jump,' yelled Pete.

My skin was still tingling. Especially under the underpants. 'It's the underpants,' I said. 'The underpants are giving me strength.' I grinned. 'They are not underpants. They are *wunderpants*.'

'Superjocks,' said Pete. We both started cackling like a couple of hens. We laughed until our sides ached.

4

I told Pete not to tell anyone about the wunderpants. We decided to keep it a secret. Nothing much happened until the cross-country race that afternoon. All the boys went to the changing room to put on their running gear. Scrag Murphy was there. I tried to get into my shorts without him seeing my wunderpants, but it was no good. He noticed them as soon as I dropped my jeans.

'Ah ha,' he shouted. 'Look at baby britches. Look at his fairy pants.' Everyone looked. They all started to laugh. How embarrassing. They were all looking at the fairies on my wunderpants.

Scrag Murphy was a big, fat bloke. He was really tough. He came over and pulled the elastic on my wunderpants. Then he let it go. 'Ouch,' I said. 'Cut that out. That hurts.'

'What's the matter, little Diddums?' he said. 'Can't you take it?' He shoved me roughly against the wall. I wasn't going to let him get away with that, so I pushed him back – just a little push. He went flying across the room and crashed into the wall on the other side. I just didn't know my own strength. That little push had sent him all that way. It was the wunderpants.

Scrag Murphy looked at me with shock and surprise that soon turned to a look of hate. But he didn't say anything. No one said anything. They were all thinking I was going to get my block knocked off next time I saw Scrag Murphy.

About forty kids were running in the race. We had to run through the countryside, following markers that had been put out by the teachers. It was a hot day, so I decided to wear a pair of shorts but no top.

As soon as the starting gun went I was off like a flash. I had kept my wunderpants on and they were working really well. I went straight out to the front.

I had never run so fast before. As I ran along the road I passed a man on a bike. He tried to keep up with me, but he couldn't. Then I passed a car. This was really something. This was great.

I looked behind. None of the others was in sight – I was miles ahead. The trail turned off the road and into the bush. I was running along a narrow track in the forest. After a while I came to a small creek. I was hot so I decided to have a dip. After all, the others were a long way behind; I had plenty of time. I took off my shorts and running shoes, but I left the wunderpants on. I wasn't going to part with them.

I dived into the cold water. It was refreshing. I lay on my back looking at the sky. Life was good. These wunderpants were terrific. I would never be scared of Scrag Murphy while I had them on.

Then something started to happen – something terrible. The wunderpants started to get tight. They hurt. They were shrinking. They were shrinking smaller and smaller. The pain was awful. I had to get them off. I struggled and wriggled; they were so tight they cut into my skin. In the end I got them off, and only just in time. They shrank so small that they would only just fit over my thumb. I had a narrow escape. I could have been killed by the shrinking wunderpants.

Just then I heard voices coming. It was the others in the race. I was trapped – I couldn't get out to put on my shorts. There were girls in the race. I had to stay in the middle of the creek in the nude.

5

It took quite a while for all the others to run by. They were all spread out along the track. Every time I went to get out of the pool, someone else would come. After a while Pete stopped at the pool. 'What are you doing?' he said. 'Even superjocks won't help you win from this far back.'

'Keep going,' I said. 'I'll tell you about it later.' I didn't want to tell him that I was in the nude. Some girls were with him.

Pete and the girls took off along the track. A bit later the last runner arrived. It was Scrag Murphy. He couldn't run fast – he was carrying too much weight. 'Well, look at this,' he said. 'It's little Fairy Pants. And what's this we have here?' He picked up my shorts and running shoes from the bank of the creek. Then he ran off with them.

'Come back,' I screamed. 'Bring those back here.' He didn't take any notice. He just laughed and kept running.

I didn't know what to do. I didn't have a stitch of clothing. I didn't even have any shoes. I was starting to feel cold; the water was freezing. I was covered in goose pimples and my teeth were chattering. In the end I had to get out. I would have frozen to death if I stayed in the water any longer.

I went and sat on a rock in the sun and tried to think of a way to get home without being seen. It was all right in the bush. I could always hide behind a tree if someone came. But once I reached the road I would be in trouble; I couldn't just walk along the road in the nude.

Then I had an idea. I looked at the tiny underpants. I couldn't put them on, but they still might work. I put them over my thumb and jumped. It was no good. It was just an ordinary small jump. I picked up a stone and threw it. It only went a short way, not much of a throw at all. The pants were too small, and I was my weak old self again.

I lay down on the rock in the sun. Ants starred to crawl over me. Then the sun went behind a cloud. I started to get cold, but I couldn't walk home – not in the raw. I felt miserable. I looked around for something to wear, but there was nothing. Just trees, bushes and grass.

I knew I would have to wait until dark. The others would all have gone home by now. Pete would think I had gone home, and my parents would think I was at his place. No one was going to come and help me.

I started to think about Scrag Murphy. He was going to pay for this. I would get him back somehow.

Time went slowly, but at last it started to grow dark. I made my way back along the track. I was in bare feet and I kept standing on stones. Branches reached out and scratched me in all sorts of painful places. Then I started to think about snakes. What if I stood on one?

There were all sorts of noises in the dark. The moon had gone in, and it was hard to see where I was going. I have to admit it: I was scared. Scared stiff. To cheer myself up I started to think about what I was going to do to Scrag Murphy. Boy, was he going to get it.

At last I came to the road. I was glad to be out of the bush. My feet were cut and bleeding and I hobbled along. Every time a car went by I had to dive into the bushes. I couldn't let myself get caught in the headlights of the cars.

I wondered what I was going to do when I reached the town. There might be people around. I broke off a branch from a bush and held it in front of my 'you know what'. It was prickly, but it was better than nothing.

By the time I reached the town it was late. There was no one around. But I had to be careful – someone might come out of a house at any minute. I ran from tree to tree and wall to wall, hiding in the shadows as I went. Lucky for me the moon was in and it was very dark.

Then I saw something that gave me an idea – a phone box. I opened the door and stepped inside. A dim light shone on my naked body. I hoped than no one was looking. I had no money, but Pete had told me that if you yell into the ear-piece they can hear you on the other end. It was worth a try. I dialled our home number. Dad answered. 'Yes,' he said.

'I'm in the nude,' I shouted. 'I've lost my clothes. Help. Help.'

'Hello, hello. Who's there?' said Dad.

I shouted at the top of my voice, but Dad just kept saying 'Hello'. He sounded cross. Then I heard him say to Mum, 'It's probably that boy up to his tricks again.' He hung up the phone.

I decided to make a run for it. It was the only way. I dropped my bush and started running. I went for my life. I reached our street without meeting a soul. I thought I was safe, but I was wrong. I crashed right into someone and sent them flying. It was old Mrs Jeeves from across the road.

'Sorry,' I said. 'Gee, I'm sorry.' I helped her stand up. She was a bit short-sighted and it was dark. She hadn't noticed that I didn't have any clothes on. Then the moon came out – the blazing moon. I tried to cover my nakedness with my hands, but it was no good.

'Disgusting,' she screeched. 'Disgusting. I'll tell your father about this.'

I ran home as fast as I could. I went in the back door and jumped into bed. I tried to pretend that I was asleep. Downstairs I could hear Mrs Jeeves yelling at Dad; then the front door closed. I heard his footsteps coming up the stairs.

6

Well, I really copped it. I was in big trouble. Dad went on and on. 'What are you thinking of, lad?

Running around in the nude. Losing all your clothes. What will the neighbours think?' He went on like that for about a week. I couldn't tell him the truth – he wouldn't believe it. No one would. The only ones who knew the whole story were Pete and I.

Dad grounded me for a month. I wasn't allowed out of the house except to go to school. No pictures, no swimming, nothing. And no pocket money either.

It was a bad month. Very bad indeed. At school Scrag Murphy gave me a hard time. He called me 'Fairy Pants'. Every one thought it was a great joke, and there was nothing I could do about it. He was just too big for me, and his mates were all tough guys.

'This is serious,' said Pete. 'We have to put Scrag Murphy back in his box. They are starting to call me "Friend of Fairy Pants" now. We have to get even.'

We thought and thought but we couldn't come up with anything. Then I remembered the mouse race in Smith's barn. 'We will win the mouse race,' I shouted. 'It's in a month's time. We can use the next month to train my mouse.'

'That's it,' said Pete. 'The prize is fifty dollars. Scrag Murphy thinks he is going to win. It will really get up his nose if we take off the prize.'

I went and fetched Swift Sam. 'He's small,' I said. 'But he's fast. I bet he can beat Murphy's mouse. It's called Mugger.'

We started to train Swift Sam. Every day after school we took him around a track in the back yard. We tied a piece of cheese on the end of a bit of string. Swift Sam chased after it as fast as he could. After six laps we gave him the piece of cheese to eat. At the start he could do six laps in ten minutes. By the end of the month he was down to three minutes.

'Scrag Murphy, look out,' said Pete with a grin. 'We are really going to beat the pants off you this time.'

7

The day of the big race came at last. There were about one hundred kids in Smith's barn. No adults knew about it – they would probably have stopped it if they knew. It cost fifty cents to get in. That's where the prize money came from. A kid called Tiger Gleeson took up the money and gave out the prize at the end. He was the organizer of the whole thing.

Scrag Murphy was there, of course. 'It's in the bag,' he swaggered. 'Mugger can't lose. I've fed him on a special diet. He is the fittest mouse in the county. He will eat Swift Sam, just you wait and see.'

I didn't say anything. But I was very keen to see his mouse, Mugger. Scrag Murphy had it in a box. No one had seen it yet.

'Right,' said Tiger. 'Get out your mice.' I put Swift Sam down on the track. He looked very small. He started sniffing around. I hoped he would run as fast with the other mice there – he hadn't had any match practice before. Then the others put their mice on the track. Everyone except Scrag Murphy. He still had Mugger in the box.

Scrag Murphy put his hand in the box and took out Mugger. He was the biggest mouse I had ever seen. He was at least ten times as big as Swift Sam. 'Hey,' said Pete. 'That's not a mouse. That's a rat. You can't race a rat. It's not fair.'

'It's not a rat,' said Scrag Murphy in a threatening voice. 'It's just a big mouse. I've been feeding it up'. I looked at it again. It was a rat all right. It was starting to attack the mice.

'We will take a vote,' said Tiger. 'All those that think it is a rat, put your hands up.' He counted all the hands.

'Fifty,' he said. 'Now all those who say that Mugger

is a mouse put your hands up.' He counted again.

'Fifty-two. Mugger is a mouse.'

Scrag Murphy and his gang started to cheer. He had brought all his mates with him. It was a put-up job.

'Right,' said Tiger Gleeson. 'Get ready to race.'

8

There were about ten mice in the race – or I should nine mice and one rat. Two rats if you counted Scrag Murphy. All the owners took out their string and cheese. 'Go,' shouted Tiger Gleeson.

Mugger jumped straight on to a little mouse next to him and bit it on the neck. The poor thing fell over and lay still. 'Boo,' yelled some of the crowd.

Swift Sam ran to the front straight away. He was going really well. Then Mugger started to catch up. It was neck and neck for five laps. First Mugger would get in front, then Swift Sam. Everyone in the barn went crazy. They were yelling their heads off.

By the sixth lap Mugger started to fall behind. All the other mice were not in the race. They had been lapped twice by Mugger and Swift Sam. But Mugger couldn't keep up with Swift Sam; he was about a tail behind. Suddenly something terrible happened. Mugger jumped on to Swift Sam's tail and grabbed it in his teeth. The crowd started to boo. Even Scrag Murphy's mates were booing.

But Swift Sam kept going. He didn't stop for a second. He just pulled that great rat along after him. It rolled over and over behind the little mouse. Mugger held on for grim death, but he couldn't stop Swift Sam. 'What a mouse,' screamed the crowd as Swift Sam crossed the finish line still towing Mugger behind him.

Scrag Murphy stormed off out of the barn. He didn't even take Mugger with him. Tiger handed me the fifty dollars. Then he held up Swift Sam. 'Swift Sam is the winner,' he said. 'The only mouse in the world with its own little pair of fairy underpants.'

Choosing a brilliant book
can be a tricky business...
but not any more

www.puffin.co.uk

The best selection of books at your fingertips

So get clicking!

Searching the site is easy – you'll find what you're looking for at the click of a mouse, from great authors to brilliant books and more!

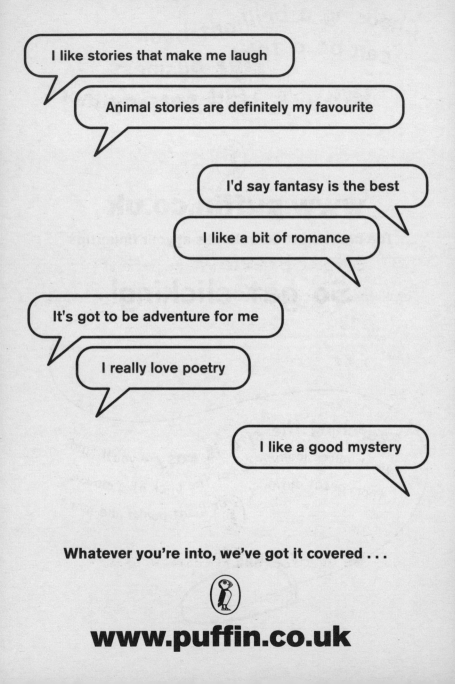

hotnews@puffin

Hot off the press!
You'll find all the latest exclusive Puffin news here

Where's it happening?
Check out our author tours and events programme

Best-sellers
What's hot and what's not? Find out in our charts

E-mail updates
Sign up to receive all the latest news
straight to your e-mail box

Links to the coolest sites
Get connected to all the best author web sites

Book of the Month
Check out our recommended reads

www.puffin.co.uk

www.puffin.co.uk.www.puffin.co.uk.www.puffin.co.uk

bookinfo.competitions.news.games.sneakpreviews

www.puffin.co.uk.www.puffin.co.uk.www.puffin.co.uk

adventure.bestsellers.fun.coollinks.freestuff

www.puffin.co.uk.www.puffin.co.uk.www.puffin.co.uk

explore.yourshout.awards.toptips.authorinfo

www.puffin.co.uk.www.puffin.co.uk.www.puffin.co.uk

greatbooks.greatbooks.greatbooks.greatbooks

www.puffin.co.uk.www.puffin.co.uk.www.puffin.co.uk

reviews.poems.jokes.authorevents.audioclips

www.puffin.co.uk.www.puffin.co.uk.www.puffin.co.uk

interviews.e-mailupdates.bookinfo.competitions.news

www.puffin.co.uk

games.sneakpreviews.adventure.bestsellers.fun

www.puffin.co.uk.www.puffin.co.uk.www.puffin.co.uk

bookinfo.competitions.news.games.sneakpreviews

www.puffin.co.uk.www.puffin.co.uk.www.puffin.co.uk

adventure.bestsellers.fun.coollinks.freestuff

www.puffin.co.uk.www.puffin.co.uk.www.puffin.co.uk

explore.yourshout.awards.toptips.authorinfo

www.puffin.co.uk.www.puffin.co.uk.www.puffin.co.uk

greatbooks.greatbooks.greatbooks.greatbooks

www.puffin.co.uk.www.puffin.co.uk.www.puffin.co.uk

reviews.poems.jokes.authorevents.audioclips

www.puffin.co.uk.www.puffin.co.uk.www.puffin.co.uk

Choosing a brilliant book
can be a tricky business...
but not any more

www.puffin.co.uk

The best selection of books at your fingertips

So get clicking!

Searching the site is easy – you'll find what you're looking for at the click of a mouse, from great authors to brilliant books and more!

Read more in Puffin

For complete information about books available from Puffin – and Penguin – and how to order them, contact us at the appropriate address below. Please note that for copyright reasons the selection of books varies from country to country.

www.puffin.co.uk

In the United Kingdom: Please write to Dept EP, Penguin Books Ltd, Bath Road, Harmondsworth, West Drayton, Middlesex UB7 ODA

In the United States: Please write to Penguin Putnam Inc., P.O. Box 12289, Dept B, Newark, New Jersey 07101–5289 or call 1–800–788–6262

In Canada: Please write to Penguin Books Canada Ltd, 10 Alcorn Avenue, Suite 300, Toronto, Ontario M4V 3B2

In Australia: Please write to Penguin Books Australia Ltd, P.O. Box 257, Ringwood, Victoria 3134

In New Zealand: Please write to Penguin Books (NZ) Ltd, Private Bag 102902, North Shore Mail Centre, Auckland 10

In India: Please write to Penguin Books India Pvt Ltd, 11 Panscheel Shopping Centre, Panscheel Park, New Delhi 110 017

In the Netherlands: Please write to Penguin Books Netherlands bv, Postbus 3507, NL–1001 AH Amsterdam

In Germany: Please write to Penguin Books Deutschland GmbH, Metzlerstrasse 26, 60594 Frankfurt am Main

In Spain: Please write to Penguin Books S. A., Bravo Murillo 19, 1° B, 28015 Madrid

In Italy: Please write to Penguin Italia s.r.l., Via Felice Casati 20, I–20124 Milano

In France: Please write to Penguin France S. A., 17 rue Lejeune, F–31000 Toulouse

In Japan: Please write to Penguin Books Japan, Ishikiribashi Building, 2–5–4, Suido, Bunkyo-ku, Tokyo 112

In South Africa: Please write to Longman Penguin Southern Africa (Pty) Ltd, Private Bag X08, Bertsham 2013